The Vampyres

Table of Contents

The Vampyres

C.R. Kane

Foreword by Tal Minear

To request permission, contact the author at:

seearcane@gmail.com.

Library of Congress Data is available.

ISBN: 979-8-218-37458-7

First Edition, February 2024

Published by C.R. Kane

A See Arcane Book

www.seearcanescribbles.com

Printed in the United States of America

This is a work of fiction. All places, events, and characters, living, dead or undead, are a product of the imagination or otherwise used fictitiously. Many of them were laboriously dug up from the graves of public domain and borrowed with the permission of their original creators by way of séance. No vampires, vampyres, or other revenants were harmed in the making of this book. Unless they had it coming.

This book is dedicated to John William Polidori for the first, to Bram Stoker for the best, and to the book clubs of Dracula Daily and Re: Dracula for the reminder of those undead I so love to loathe.

Foreword

Vampire stories have had a stranglehold on us since their first appearance in literature. From, "The Vampyre," to *Dracula*, these creatures of the night have haunted our collective imagination for over a hundred years and still fascinate in the present day. I can testify to being a card-carrying member of the Dracula Daily online book club, where we read the novel as it happens in the chronological order of everyone's journal entries. I even got a bit carried away and made an audio drama with the same premise, Re: Dracula. A whole community has sprung up to enjoy the novel together; a community in which I got to meet C.R. Kane.

Beyond diving into this old story afresh, many have taken to their own versions of sequels. To each their own opinion, but personally I've yet to find a sequel that really works for me. Stories *inspired* by *Dracula,* however? I'll eat those right up. Kane's work has a Draculaen influence, but they approach the vampiric with their own twist. It's part deliciously morbid, part grippingly romantic, part "I don't know what that is, but those teeth are staying *away*." *The Vampyres* is an excellent addition to the contemporary gothic genre, and also my nightmares. Like all the rest of Kane's writing, it sits with me long after I'm done.

Is this story a sequel to *Dracula*, you might ask? Calling it such feels like a disservice, and this is coming from someone who holds the novel very dear. Perhaps that's because Dracula, while mentioned in the story, looms in the distance. We're not here to follow up on the Count. The story is focused on someone, some*thing* else. Something that's out to give the world's living dead a reason to run very far, very fast.

The Vampyres imagines vampirism used as a sort of contract to dodge death, which I think is a fascinating way to interpret it. What kind of person would choose to prey on their kind for immortality? Who would seek to wheel and deal with life itself? For an answer, the story puts us in the shoes of such a dealmaker. Living forever makes names a bit fluid, but we'll call him Gordon.

As a reader, you're stuck in his head, and that almost makes you want to root for him. He's the main character, after all. But... he kind of sucks (pun intended). Gordon is mean and ruthless and relishes the suffering of others. You're almost held hostage in his repugnant thoughts. When things start to go wrong for him, you feel a conflict. You want Gordon to understand what's happening so that you can piece everything together, but solving that puzzle means he might escape the consequences of his crimes. Which you don't want, of course...but you also want to know *what the heck is going on.*

As with *Dracula*, understanding the antagonist is a vital part of the narrative, even if the roles of both hunted and hunter have been taken by monsters. There are a ton of hidden connections to be uncovered between the veins of this story and *Dracula's* old blood, and they're too fun for me to spoil. You don't *need* to have read Stoker's work first, but if you haven't, you should give it a read after (I know a book club you could join).

At its undead heart, under the fangs and bloodshed and requisite supernatural trappings, *The Vampyres* explores the cost of an oath. We all make small promises we don't plan to keep. Or big promises we say for dramatic effect. Contracts made in passion, not just the cold blood of Faustian rituals. What if you were held to them? You *swore* you would do it, so do it you must. *Is it not so?* The living, the dead, and those in-between hold you to your word. Among stronger forces. Older ones. Powers that can't be stopped by stake or steel or the turn of time.

Under the thumb of such an influence, when time itself is meaningless, what has meaning? What would you do if you planned to live forever? How is humanity warped when no longer tied to a human lifespan? I'm asking you questions I'm not going to answer, because I want you to hold these in your mind as you read. There's a mystery in the waiting pages, and perhaps these ruminations will help you unravel it. A mountain of revelations is waiting to pounce on the Vampyres themselves. Here's hoping you weather them better than they do.

Just remember to keep the lights on.

And never invite a stranger past the threshold.

Happy reading!

TAL MINEAR

The Coffin Opens...

I'm writing this at the far end of June, counting down the days and nights until my good friend and favorite menaced solicitor, Jonathan Harker, must escape Castle Dracula or die trying.

It's the second year in a row I'll be doing so, waiting in wonderful, dreadful anticipation with a legion of fellow readers of Matt Kirkland's popular Substack, *Dracula Daily*. I'm waiting with double the eagerness since this massive online book club has been joined by the audio accompaniment of the podcast *Re: Dracula*, which follows the same rule as the Substack: Each dated entry of Bram Stoker's *Dracula* is fed to us on the same day of the calendar. No chapters, only chronological journal entries, diary recitations, news clippings, business papers, and the logs of doomed characters stretched out across almost half a year of classic gothic horror goodness. It's introduced many new readers to a novel that they only knew by name and the tangential—and, let's be frank, consistently unfaithful—adaptations and spinoffs in media.

For others who are already ravenous fans of the book, it provides a tidal wave of vindication and camaraderie as the richness of the original novel is resurrected from the dust and atrophy of more than a century's worth of neglect.

'Look! Look at everything you've been missing! Look at how amazing the characters are! Look at how terrifying Dracula is! Look at all the plots and themes and groundbreaking genre goings-on that have been smothered for 127 years to make way for endless vampiric bodice ripper thrillers with the cast's names loosely pinned on!'

These days, I can claim to be one of those readers and/or listeners. But back when I first dipped my toes into *Dracula Daily*, I was doing it as someone hovering in-between the new and old readers. I recalled having read *Dracula* before, ages ago. I owned the novel! But, as many of the readers in the Substack will point out, devouring a book in one sitting is a very different thing from metaphorically joining hands with the characters within and waiting through every.

Single. Day. And week. And month.

Soaking in the passage of time, the ramifications of the threat, and the precedent of the insidious bloodstained powers in play with true appreciation, rather than rushing through and ticking mental boxes for Scary Tropes™ that the average 21st century horror hound is desensitized to. Many of said tropes being either invented or perfected in Stoker's masterpiece outright.

All of which is a very long way of saying that I would not have gone off the undead deep end if not for the experience that Matt Kirkland and so many new friends in the Dusty Old Gothic Classics Club have given me. Because Count Dracula not only took me by the throat, but chucked me straight out the window like a shaving mirror and sent me into a spiraling dive through so many other terrifying supernatural tales I'd alternately forgotten about in a high school haze or else never encountered before.

It was between updates from the Substack that I began snapping up other horror stories of old to fill the void. In doing so, I ran into some fantastic fanged faces far older than the Count's, among other paranormal parasites. I read, I reread, I picked literary bones clean in short stories and novellas and then did the same again for *Dracula* as its pieces funneled in across the calendar.

And then, come November, there was no more to read.

Just a coffin full of ashes, its lid shut in tandem with the book cover.

But if there's one thing ashes are good for, it's providing fertile ground to grow something new. Especially when stirred in with the grislier fodder of meticulous what-ifs and analyses that had cropped up while going over the novel and its predecessor bloodsucking bogeymen stories with a magnifying glass. An abundance of possibilities flowered from that rich old foundation and scratched my mental itch with their premises. But they also began to frustrate with one vital question:

'Hey, who's going to write this so I can enjoy it?'

A question that would go on to precede numerous outlines and drafts for likewise numerous tales grown from scenarios dreamt up in the interim between doses of *Dracula* past and present. One of which is the story you're about to read.

It features some characters you can recognize from your classic collections of supernatural horror, regardless of what aliases they wear. As well as some who might need a double-take before they come into focus. Between them is a worrisome rise of cadaverous carnage, some curious cohabitation, and a close look at the nature of death, undeath, immortality, and the precarious routes a body can take to all three. Whether they want to or not.

I wrote this for me. I wrote this for characters I adore and who I adore tormenting with new terrors. I wrote this for anyone out there who likes breaking well-trod narrative ground into jigsaw puzzles and making unexpected pieces fit together. I wrote this for the friends I've made on the trek to shadow-haunted mountains, to moonlit Victorian streets, and back again, all of us reveling in the sincerity of fear and love that seems so tricky to find in present fiction. But beyond all that, I wrote this to answer another question that was never quite addressed.

Once upon a time, a man declared he would sell his soul to send another to Hell. Considering all the events that transpired after, it made me wonder:

Did the sale go through?

"Why, this is Hell, nor am I out of it
Think'st thou that I who saw the face of God
And tasted the eternal joys of Heaven
Am not tormented with ten thousand hells
In being deprived of everlasting bliss?
O Faustus, leave these frivolous demands
Which strikes a terror to my fainting soul!"
—Christopher Marlowe, *Doctor Faustus*

"Help, Heaven, help and favour her!
Child, utter an Ave Marie!
Wise and great are the doings of God;
He loves and pities thee."
"Out, mother, out on the empty lie!
Doth he heed my despair, —doth he list to my cry?
What boots it now to hope or to pray?
The night is come, —there is no more day."
—Gottfried August Bürger, *Lenore*

All our times have come
Here but now they're gone
Seasons don't fear the reaper
Nor do the wind, the sun or the rain
We can be like they are
Come on, baby (don't fear the reaper)
Baby, take my hand (don't fear the reaper)
We'll be able to fly (don't fear the reaper)
Baby, I'm your man
—Blue Öyster Cult, "Don't Fear the Reaper"

I

The phone came alive at midnight. A fact he would only become aware of well after two in the morning. He followed at least one form of etiquette at the table by silencing the device for the duration of each game. He broke no rules in any casino, however polished or derelict. It was what preserved his hobby. The gambling itself he could take or leave, but the players themselves were excellent sport.

He beggared the starved and bloodshot player hoping to win funds enough to live off for a month, then played as if blind in order to lose it all to whoever needed the winnings least. Considering how equal the misfortune spread across the board for any who played with him, be they rich or poor, saintly spirit or giddy sinner, it was rarely too long before even the least credulous in his circles began to shiver when he showed his face. Or so it was in less congested metropolises where the cattle weren't so bombarded with other distractions that they couldn't recognize an ill omen when he took a seat at the felted table. It remained true now, as always, that whoever played against him never got far from the table without misery and worse crashing down on them. Some wound up penniless, withering to nothing. Others found themselves cursed with unthinkable misfortune the moment they spent his money, blighted by some medley of bankruptcy, illness, prison, madness and fatality.

The result was always a pleasant surprise to him. Results that so many of the herd never bothered to notice even in this age of conspiracy and wildfire gossip living in their myriad screens. Bless their blunted little souls.

That night he was feeling more at ease than he had in some weeks. Even one of the cocktail girls, whose mind carried a pleasing well of empathy and whose fingernails were still lined with soil from a group tree planting, tickled at his peripheral senses and twitched his appetite awake. If he wanted, he could talk a phone number out of her over a drink he would never choke down, perhaps keeping her pinned at a stool with his face and his wallet. He might dance her along for a date or three and then bite her throat out before they struck June. The same could be said for the svelte young man behind the bar who had almost fumbled his showman mixologist pour upon making eye contact with him. He had a tang of hope and action sweating from him, the kind that was destined either to make a hero or a martyr of him someday. It would almost be a mercy to put him down in his prime.

The girl, then.

He flung a little mental nudge her way. Enough to make her turn her head. At the same time, he fished out the phone to play with. Just to have it ready should the exchange come quicker than anticipated. A small mountain of text messages sat fresh and unread there. This was surprising on its own, considering how scant his contacts were. Then he saw the name. Irritation broke across his mood like a rash.

He quit the current table and took himself to a private corner to read. Irritation grew into something heavier. Sicker.

At the bottom of the reading, he tapped play so he could watch.

When all was seen and heard, his hand twitched and crunched in the phone's sides. Spider web cracks flew across the screen. A ruddy gentleman stopped en route to the toilet in time to see this and mumbled something about how he ought to invest in a device of higher quality. The man had a cousin working for a new startup, you see, and if he was so inclined—

His last mote of joy that night was the look on that rubicund face as it met the eyes of something no longer bothering to pretend it was human. A grey eye might be ignored. Not so for a dead one. He left the man scrambling off to the stalls.

On his way to the doors, he made sure to radiate every deathly ounce of his presence into the air. A quelling cold that made the glee of the night's winners crumble into a dread of things they could not name. Then he was out and under the moon. He nursed from that pale wedge in desperate reflex. It was such a thin taste here, lost in the searing pollution of streetlights and neon, but he basked just the same. Still basking, he crushed the phone in his fist and dropped the remains down a sewer grate.

Then he was gone, one of a thousand streaks of rolling light and metal in the dark.

II

He only ever carried phones as a prop.

In this age and those to follow, it would be imperative to keep one of the aggravating little slabs on hand for the purposes of engaging in the back-and-forth patter that so many of the cattle insisted on in those hours when they weren't side by side. Fortunately, he'd found himself blessed enough to dodge one of the maladies which others indulging in a healthy unlife hadn't.

Some poor bastards had started out having to walk around without reflections or shadows while grumbling over the barriers of running water and uninvited thresholds. Others only discovered their drawbacks as the 20th century budded. It was quickly revealed that their photographs came out either empty or hideously distorted. Audio of their voices came out muted or garbled into static. He'd avoided all of these tells by trading for a less endowed state of undeath rather than glutting himself on all the powerful options in reach. His variation still came with the most desired prize without any need for occult filigree.

Given blood and moonlight enough, there was no mode of death from which he could not rebound. Same as any of the self-made devils lurking about in the shadows. Such shadows that were left for things like them. In a lighter mood, he might have enjoyed the notion of picking at the wounds of those who'd not bothered with the foresight of arranging investments and back doors of identification for the centuries to come.

Only fools could miss how tight the noose of bureaucracy was becoming. An ageless body loitering among mayfly mortals had to be prepared and he had once laughed to himself at how the sorcerous types gnashed their fangs and scrambled to cover themselves as time ticked on and their lounging hedonism softened into corrosion.

But such amusing thoughts had iced over in recent decades. He had not gotten as far as he had alive or undead by resting on his laurels. Oh, he might enjoy playing with his food and sowing a bit of casual desolation where it could be nurtured, but he never gambled when it came to things that might inconvenience him. Things like other bloodsuckers, for instance.

A few had been proper nuisances of old. The majority of the stray vampiric beauties wandering around random crypts and lonely midnights to lure gullible lovers into their teeth were invariably the result of irresponsible collecting by the usual harem hoarders. Such carelessness often led to sleeping cadavers staked and slaughtered in their boxes. Not a concern for himself, naturally—he could enjoy a bed rather than graveyard dirt or casket walls—but the attention itself got too many hackles up.

Enough hackles raised about a certain type of person could lead to inconvenience. One of his oldest worries was the notion of an outright arrest. A trial. A boxing away into a great stone cage of a prison where he would have no choice but to resort to his teeth rather than his daggers and risk being found out as a perpetually young and deathless inmate. A bloody break out, an escape, some secret place where he could lay under the moon and heal from the bullets, going on the run for a decades-long stint until all assumed he must be dead; all these he could picture, but would rather avoid. Hence the need for cannier sorts with this unique condition. Those who knew how to take their fun and feeding between the lines of human living and laws.

It was not against the law that certain formerly-benign persons around you turned apoplectic with insanity, horror, or rage after spending a few months in your company. Nor was it against the law to stamp someone's empty little head with the inorganic impression of infatuation so that they, like insects drawn to the pitcher plant, would come within reach willingly. There was no law against trances and the mystic weight of locking an unwitting brain into an oath with more power to it than hollow words, no more than there were laws against having a seventh sense of awareness when it came to the makeup of a soul.

And, apart from those silly backwards places where superstition still hobbled, there was certainly no law against being an accused vampire. Or a vampyre, to go by his preferred spelling. Kate Northcott mocked him for this and other affectations on those sparse occasions when they met.

Her name was not Kate Northcott any more than his was Gordon Williams, but it remained the name she was most attached to. It had history.

"I turned into a proper ghost story with it in the 1880s. Back when the mesmerist fad was booming, you know. Popped one little stage magician's blood vessel right there in the middle of his act." A slim finger waggled. "I take offense to people playing with my toys. It's his own fault for trying to walk my poor John around."

Her poor John who had, like every beau before him, been told the exact nature of both their lovely cruel Kate's needs and precisely what she intended to do with them should they go through with marriage and life thereafter. More, that she would see them dead if they abandoned her. Each man had run. Each had died. Perhaps they'd have lasted longer if she ever allowed a trip to the altar before laying out the truth post-honeymoon, but the rules of her own contract demanded the revelation come before any wedding bells. Not a terrible bargain, all things considered.

This in mind, he had posited that she might have better luck keeping a paramour if she used her fine senses to detect one of those lot who would trip over their own aching members for the chance to be an eternal puppet to her psychic appetite. Miss Northcott had batted her lashes. As always, the lambent shine of her eyes tried to work their magic on his own will. As always, they'd scrabbled for a grip on the frictionless wall that shielded his mind from such parasites, be they dead drinkers of blood, soul, or otherwise. She'd huffed and tittered after the expected failure.

"Now what's the point if they *want* it? I don't see *you* jumping at the sea of willing victims hoping for unlife eternal draped in your arms at the cost of a hickey and a liquid diet. You could have had a set of twins that one time, no? The brother and sister, whoever they were. The Audreys? The Ambers?"

"The appetizers," he said with all the pining recollection of an epicure mourning an immaculately supple steak. "They were a pleasant distraction. It's the most any meal should aspire to." So saying, he made a point of revealing one of the daggers he still kept on his person. Antique and bejeweled, he took some small pride in keeping the whole set gleaming and up to the task whenever the latest game came to an end. He'd admired the dead grey of his stare reflected in the steel. "I have no interest in collecting sycophants."

"Likewise." Kate had punctuated this with a dainty sip from her cup. Purposefully, he thought. The better to display that she was capable of consuming more than the spirit of a collared victim. Whether she could taste anything the café had to offer was not a topic he was interested enough to pry for. "But that begs the question of why you're suddenly so concerned for your fellows that you would bother with the hardship of social interaction to pass your little warning on."

Gordon regarded her stonily over his untouched plate.

"I'm not concerned for any of our 'fellows' any more than I'm concerned for you. I have every belief that I am one of the least endangered of our kind and all its branches by dint of having some amount of grey matter dedicated to not flaunting my reality. At most, I give you credit for being canny enough to dwell within plausible deniability with your methods. More importantly, you should have senses enough to glean for yourself if this threat is in your midst. Likewise enough intelligence to enlist others for help with culling it."

Kate picked at her croissant.

"Even if I believed you would exert effort to come to my aid, I still fail to see what threat you've conjured to be afraid of. Your only evidence so far is that you haven't been in touch with the others of the old guard in some time. Most have never been keen on communication and the last I checked, the bulk of them prefer staying sedentary rather than pursuing our migratory lifestyle. Castles and manors and villages turned into necropolises and so on. Hermit types by nature."

"Hermits would be at home," Gordon countered. The dagger twisted in his hand. "All the places I've visited have been empty. And filled with dust."

She had frowned up at him.

"Dust..?"

"Dust and growth. There were flowers growing in those messes that were fresh enough in their conversions to have flesh leftover.

Compost." He thought back to the surreal gardens left behind in that sequestered corner of Munich that once belonged to Dolingen. Then of a Serbian village that had been swallowed by a ravenously loving pack of wurdulacs, stopped short of virulence by their rules of homeland borders. Among others. Dust in piles, dust wearing ancient clothes, dust in coffins. Scattered throughout were the bounty of younger fledglings. Meat and bone converted to soil from which wild roses, ash trees, and garlic sprouted in healthy crops. As for the nobler estates?

"The chateaus and mansions are abandoned now. Passed on to the wealthy living or standing as museum pieces. *Maybe* their former masters left it all behind in the past hundred or so years to dodge modern scrutiny of the family tree. I'd like to think so. Just as I'd like to think there was a less worrisome reason that all the pseudonyms and auxiliary domains I tried to follow up on had no recognizable owners when I checked in on them. But even if I were dense enough to convince myself of such, there's at least one case that suggests—,"

"The Carpathians." Kate beamed at him and his stunted sermon. "The castle in the mountains has been fully gutted since 1897, dear. Looted and halfway dismantled to the foundation by the locals. What's left of it is there for the tourists." She patted his knuckles gently. "If you're worried about the handsy old boyar, don't be. He's been mobbed and murdered before. A shame about his girls in their boxes, but they *were* only born of a bite, poor things. No contractual resurrection to fall back on. That Count, if he is still bothering with being a Count, is doubtlessly off haunting some contemporary castle someplace. Probably a nice high rise for him to skitter down or make his batty flights from. Just as the other oldies have likely taken themselves to higher ground. And if their minions really have run afoul of some sterling sorts with hammer, stake, and axe? There's always more pretty chattel to choose from."

Her laugh was a brittle crystalline sound.

"Honestly, I'm shocked that you'd be the one to turn jumpy over such a thing. Supposing there was some active force in the world bumping the lower tier wraiths off, it would still be no more than an annoyance for us. We've both had our share of murders to prove as much. The dried-up old conqueror certainly had his fill in the warlord days, if I don't mistake the legends."

"He did," Gordon granted. "And he *has* reassembled himself many times before. Which is my point. Supposing he is undead and active today, or was over a hundred years prior, why would he let the peasants harvest his fortress down into a ruin?"

"He's obviously ditched the place. It was a third ruined already, as I recall. I expect he washed his hands of the old rock pile." Kate shrugged at him as her attention gravitated down to her phone. A manicured thumb tapped and scrolled. More of appetite than apprehension lived in her gaze. "You can only pass yourself off as your own descendant so long before things start getting sticky anyway. Everyone hits the point where you have to get on with setting up elsewhere. And really, the warlord days *are* ancient history.

"If he'd gone out with a flourish of a massacre on the towns squirming under his eye, it would only have gotten him more unwanted attention. I recommend you start trawling through top mogul names and see if you can't spot his picture lurking in there, gone fat and happy slurping up interns." Her lips pursed. "Supposing he was one of the lucky sorts who can *have* a photo taken."

With that, the topic had died. Gordon managed to sit through another quarter of an hour in which Kate lamented the double-edged factor of her electronic allergy, woeful at never having a decent photo to spare for social media or dating apps, but likewise glad of the identity-baffling glamour it leant.

Chirpily, she reminded him that even those who grew suspicious of her would never be able to take a reliable photo or video of anything but a spectral horror with mist for eyes, unlike *some*. Better still, no one even spoke on the phone anymore. Bless texting.

He held on until she started regaling him with talk of her latest doomed darling. One Quinn Morse, the mortuary assistant who she had met in the before and after of her latest fiancé's funeral, may he rest in pieces. Mr. Morse was apparently a scrumptious treat to the psychic palate. He had proven so pleasant a distraction she might not even bother goosing his mind into vomiting out a proposal. Not for a while anyway. Why, she may even take up two-timing the boy just to snack on a groom behind his back, ha ha.

Gordon left without wishing her bon appétit.

He picked out a young couple on his way back to the train. Mister and Missus would be found folded inside a dumpster later that evening, chests carved and throats torn. A rejuvenating bout of gluttony that only gave him new energy with which to curse the lack of answers he sat with and the lack of competent allies to make up for the deficit. For a while longer he strained to lower his suspicions to the level of Miss Northcott's confidence. His main concern was so implausible as to border on impossible, after all.

The *turned* might be slain, it was true. But those who had commissioned their states from their devil or deity of choice were immune to total destruction by any of the cattle, no matter how endowed in strength or holy accoutrement.

Days and nights were spent rereading these facts in the volumes that still traveled with him to whatever land or identity he haunted. They remained preciously stored in enhanced safes as the centuries ticked on, now handled only with silk gloves and the most delicate turns of cover and page. He scoured the old tongues and took as much solace as he could from the facts laid in their script.

His contract was one of perpetual function. So long as he drank his dose of blood, he would go on forever. So long as his dead skin was grazed by moonlight, he would shed any injury or temporary death. So long as he was the thing he was, no act of man would have the power to permanently unmake him.

All these were still maintained. He was safe. As anyone else at his level or higher would be. The more grandiose warlocks and dealmakers who'd glutted themselves on fearsome add-ons available to other forms of revenant had simply moved on and were going about their business elsewhere, under new names. Of course. Of course.

"Of course," he murmured to the yellowed pages. "They all just happened to do so within the last century. On a whim."

It could be, couldn't it? Technology and the microscopic examinations of increasingly thorough systems surrounding properties and owners thereof would make it necessary to move on from old roosts sooner or later.

"Without taking any measures to preserve their estates."

And what of the villages? The ones full of living peasantry gleefully peeling the properties down to floorboards. The dead spaces where only silence and specific warding flora bloomed. What sense was there to those, if not the fact that something had been and gone and torn the masters of the land out by their bloody roots?

Something.

That was the prospect that worried him most. *Something* coming to call, *something* culling the undead and undying, *something* roaming across borders of land and water to pick them off year by year, decade by decade. *Something* that may have been active since the boyar in the mountains disappeared. *Something* which was not human and so did not fall within the parameters of their sundry pacts' protection.

Gordon grimaced. It *would* come down to a technicality, wouldn't it? Be they gods or demons or Folk in-between, there was always some damned loophole built in to ensure a trade was never quite as advertised. Gordon had studied and sworn to and dealt with a god wearing the aspect of one of those horrors which passed for divinities in the Mediterranean. One of tripled faces, of lunar light, of words stitched with power. After so many centuries, he had dared to become complacent enough to think he'd gotten away with an impenetrable exchange.

But now came this worrisome era in which all those dead who lived off the living were dropping out of sight. He might have dared to make an inquiry to Powers beyond mortal matter if he weren't afraid that this culling was the work of said Powers in the first place. Terminating contracts, as it were. Even if this weren't the case, what more did he have left to barter with for protection from...

From what?

He continued not to know and the books continued not to say. The result left him twisting unhappily between throes of frustration at his ignorance and grimmer fear of illumination that might come in the shape of his own disappearance.

As always, the cure for his despondency was to share it with others. Hence the casino. The brief high that had almost transfigured into relief.

And then had come the texts from 'N.'

Even with the phone safely demolished and abandoned, its final bleak gift stayed branded behind his eyes, searing through his thoughts awake or asleep. The first message had come at ten past midnight:

R. Need help. My arm's going black. The knife, it

A lull followed. The next message at 12:15 AM:

It's real. He's here and he's real. Quinn Morse was a cover. I can't find any of his pictures in the album now. He replaced everything with their markers. All of them.

Another lull. 12:22 AM:

Pick up, damn it! This isn't a joke! He's got all the doors and windows cut off and the police won't be here in time! I already tried to put him down, but he just keeps going. I can't drink him. I can't even hold him. He knew he knew the whole time he

Lull. 12:30 AM:

Pick up you bastard

12:31 AM:

Please, R, he's outside. He's got my arm. What's left of my arm. The door's breaking and h

12:41 AM. A video.

The clearest thing throughout the few endless minutes was the background. A plush bedroom stood out in crisp relief compared to the two figures moving in it. One was a vaguely female haze that Gordon recognized as what was left of Kate Northcott. She flickered in and out of the camera's concept of her reality. One moment she was spectral fog made of hunger and venom. In the next, she was something far more tangible and suffering for it.

Each flicker revealed a new stage of decomposition twitching in a bloodied sundress. Only one arm was left to flail with as the right was missing, swinging only a necrotic stump at the shoulder. The rest of the body followed suit between spasms. Sometimes a glottal noise that could pass for a voice broke through the static. What had been crystal was now a shrill and dwindling rasp. Dimly, Gordon thought it was strange the noise was not wetter—his cuisine almost always gurgled when enduring the kind of wound he saw staining her breast.

A crimson slit had opened where her heart would be. Her remaining hand alternated between scrabbling at it and trying to wave off the shape throwing its shadow over her from outside the borders of the screen. As she tried to kick herself back along the floor, the reason for her scuttling along the imported rug was made clear: a bullet hole had gone through one knee. The knee itself was now almost obliterated with decay while the calf and thigh were going hideously spongy. Much like the rest of her.

The last noise she made was as close to a scream that a throat of dust could manage—

"*Quin*—,"

—before a flash of silver-white swept down. It flew in a shining arc from the upper corner of the screen and through the hazy shriveled stem that had been a neck. A moment later there was no haze left. Only the corpse of the thing known as Kate Northcott collapsing in two pieces. Most of it flopped to the floor with a gruesome rattle. Her head tumbled away until it struck the nightstand, the lush tresses now a mass of grizzled cobwebs. When it stilled, the sockets revealed that the eyes had dried away to nothing.

Then Quinn Morse stepped into frame.

If Miss Northcott was mist, her killer was a ghost. The impression of a man smeared just out of true.

Really, it was the impression of a character; some escapee from a folk legend or a graphic novel. A strange blurred mesh of huntsman and mourner. Sheathed in black, Gordon could pick out suggestions of both the late Victorian and the fantasy of the American adventurer in his attire. Or perhaps he was assuming too much by the hints beneath the hanging duster and the broad brim of a hat dark as charcoal. The only things not some shade of ink were the white fall of hair growing from under the hat in wild drapes and the eyes floating in the shadowed void where a face should be. Not red, but a sickening grey that might have matched Gordon's own apart from how they burned.

He thought of cats. He thought of foxes. He thought of carrion birds.

He thought of coins not unlike the pair Quinn Morse held up in his gloved fingers. Gold pinched in old leather. They shined just as bright as the long blade gripped in the opposite hand, its helping of blood still dripping.

Gordon watched with the camera as Quinn Morse popped the coins into each of the eye sockets. A bundle of familiar blossoms and sprigs appeared from the dark mass of the coat. This was tucked neatly into the head's sagging maw as if arranging a bouquet. Quinn Morse stepped out of sight. The video ended.

A final text message appeared the instant the show finished:

My God, my God! Look not so fierce upon me! Adders and serpents, let me breathe awhile! Ugly Hell, gape not! Come not Lucifer! I'll burn my books!—O Mephistopheles!

He had wanted to laugh. To roll his eyes. To make himself tap out a reply in mocking returned verse. To inform Mr. Morse that he was lacking for proper material to parrot, especially in assuming his gods and devils brushed anywhere near something so young and gaudy as the Abrahamic.

He could. He would.

But somehow he had found himself crumpling the phone to shrapnel and racing home to start clearing out his necessities for a trip to distant quarters. He kept more than one residence as a rule whenever he wasn't taking one of his gourmand tours. A fact Kate Northcott may have known, but not well enough to have learned his other addresses. Or names.

Gordon Williams was thrown away that night.

Mason Darvell greeted the morning.

III

The shift from one estate to another was a comparatively easy one. If not because he was packed and ready to move at a moment's notice, then for the fact that there was little of importance to take. The book safe was always prepared, carefully insulated with documentation needed for sundry identities. Clothes and toiletries. Devices. A case of cards, dice, and chips. A weightier case in which his best blades were sheathed in a row. Currency for six countries. But as to furnishings?

Mason Darvell was a man of spartan living. He had a bed. He had a chair to sit in when he forced himself to stare at the television for an hour a day, gleaning as many points of interest in humanity's trudging as he could stomach in case future conversation might require it. The spiders had more impressive accommodations in the ceiling corners and kitchen cupboards. More proud investment in them too.

Which was just as well. Even when he was a living man, he'd found in himself a great unvarnished chasm where interest in his home ought to be. He *had* interests, of course. Himself. How he might inflict himself on the world as best and brutally as could be managed. How to do so for as long and painlessly as possible on his part. On noting his prized possessions, he might see how a snoop would assume a genuine love of gambling, perhaps a hobby in collecting the works of classic bladesmiths. These were simple enough things to pretend when pressed. But even when past lovers and assumed friends had given presents tied to these few flints of pleasure, they almost inevitably turned up in a pawnbroker's hands.

The interior of his soul was stark and so the walls were stark with it.

His only flourish was the hanging of heavy drapes to smother every window. A ghost of damask stained them like elaborate splashes of wine. They were velvety and opaque and kept any space he called home a perfect box of midnight at all hours.

Said drapes had their siblings already hanging in the windows of the waiting house when he arrived. It was precisely as barren as he'd left it, bar the naked mattress in its old four-poster frame. This he beat the dust from and swaddled in the bedding left vacuum-sealed in the linen closet. For almost a month he refused to stir from that bed, sometimes going whole days and nights without leaving it or the circle of tomes he combed for an explanation of the thing called Quinn Morse.

The thing that had fooled Kate Northcott, one of the most adept spiritual vampires Mason had ever encountered, into thinking it was a man. A thing that had gone out of its way to erase photographs of itself. *Him*self.

"Glamour," Mason croaked as he scratched out new notes. "Or a borrowed skin." Perhaps someone's familiar? He thought drearily of the rancid old codger who'd made a name for himself up in Sweden. Magnus. Another count numbered among the undead, if ironically bereft of the need to quaff blood to keep ticking. Alive, he had been a brute. After, he had his familiar, a squirming boneless thing in a hood, turn sadism into an artform. Mason had crossed him and the otherworldly companion before.

The man was a bit of a snob. One who put up his nose at the thought of actually greasing his hands with human gristle when he could have professionals do it for him in expert fashion.

"Unless it comes down to sacrifice," Magnus had huffed while Mason, then an Alexander, supped on the younger brother left behind by the familiar's latest assignment. The elder might have groveled to trade places, considering the state of the man's face afterwards—assuming one could call that raw slab of peeled muscle and bone a face anymore. "A sacrifice has rules, as you know. Distinct statutes set forth by the blackest Powers that must be followed to the furthest end of acquiescence. To fail in that is to risk either the loss of the pact or the ire of the called-upon party. But in any other case, those of status should really leave it to the proficient." A sidelong glance had slithered down to where Alexander was removing the Adam's apple to suckle. His nose wrinkled, adding an extra level of grotesquerie to an already unflattering countenance. "*Milord.*"

Mason who was Alexander had offered no comment. Magnus himself scarcely held his attention as much as the familiar. The familiar, already spent on its order of violence, had slithered up on a bough to watch and wait. Clinging rigidly as a tensed muscle, it clutched at the gnarled tree and showed as much expression of dull impatience as concentrated abomination could produce. Mason had assumed at the time that it was waiting to see if its master would order it to attack him as he dined. Perhaps that was part of it.

But the horrid stare shined far brighter when, as Magnus' attention moved elsewhere in his monologue, the thing glowered at the old man with a sort of leering avarice. The gash of its mouth drooled in eager rivulets. It saw Mason seeing this. Though lidless, one of the assorted bulbous eyes seemed like it wanted to wink.

In the end, they had parted cordially enough. Neither had given the other any form of contact, both seemingly aware that each possessed means of sniffing out a target as needed. The obituary of an unfortunate Mr. Wraxwall detailed how easy a thing it was on Magnus' end to track a man. Likewise for no small number of bodies in Mason's past. One didn't become such things as them without being able to hunt.

Mason's own senses had drawn him to this specific hideaway as it was the home nearest to the Braintree district. The most insidious of the deathless were still prone to sentimentality on some points, even beyond the reuse of names. In Count Magnus' case, the vile ancient often made a habit of circling back to muse over the site of Mr. Wraxwall's unhappy departure from the mortal coil.

"I will say this for the fool," Magnus had hummed in as close to a warm tone as he could muster, "he may have roused me from my latest drowse at the time, but he did do me the service of making me aware that some dullards had padlocked me in my sarcophagus. More, he was the first one to say in all my years that he wished to meet me. A toast to the little Englishman."

So they had toasted with glasses brimming with red. Claret for him, something warmer for Mason. The familiar took nothing. Only waited. And watched.

Whatever Quinn Morse was, perhaps Magnus' wretched creature and its abilities were enough of a ward to keep him at bay. Supposing it wasn't Magnus himself who'd conjured him up.

"No. No, I don't believe so," Mason murmured to the dark. It was too out of tune with the man's preferences. Miss Northcott had the grace period of a false romance. The remains of other solitaries and villages alike had been culled with a seeming tidiness that didn't pair with the meatier torments the familiar visited on its prey. Plus, there were the parting gifts to consider. The flora of folklore and the Ferryman coins. Whether Quinn Morse was his own entity or a hired horror, he wasn't following Magnus' penchants.

Mason reached his mind out and confirmed again, twice, thrice, that the man was still in his holidaying locale near Belchamp St. Paul. This was as far as confirmation could reach as, by means frustratingly obscure to Mason, the withered bastard had also secured a way to shield himself against the notice of mortal busybody systems that demanded infinite details to permit an untroubled place in civilization. There was no doubt he'd blanked the entire country manse out of the public consciousness so that he and his infernal servant could lurk unbothered. But that also meant there were no means to call ahead. It would be a surprise visit.

Mason thought again of the treatment Count Magnus reserved for those who mucked about on his property uninvited. Perhaps it was best that he bring a tithe. A little sport for the familiar to chew on for his viewing pleasure. That combined with the bait of a threat to those who'd bargained for an immunity to death would be enough.

Probably.

He was still pondering these particulars when sleep put him down.

There was a dream. A sour one. Flashes of copper, silver, and gold. Screaming. An unspeakable ululating noise that only the most charitable ear could register as a laugh. Darkness watching him with molten eyes. Mason would succeed in shaking most of it from his head by the time he left, bar the stare burning in the gloom.

It stung behind his eyelids for the rest of the day.

IV

Local fare would be the easiest to acquire, he thought.

Between his face and his tongue, Mason Darvell could draw plenty of potential candidates with or without an effort. There were several appreciating looks from those who thought he couldn't see them and as many blushes when he plied the gawkers with conversation. Yet none approached that he could work with. Too many were out and about in groups to get away with separating one from the herd. Playing the role of tourist seeking recommendations and directions was an easy enough ploy to garner interest, but no willing solo guides. He wasted an empty breath to sigh over the lack of trust found in today's livestock. True crime series and an addiction to sensationalized deaths in the news had put a deep dent in his preferred methods.

That was, the beguiling, ruining, and slaughtering of a chosen paramour the way a butcher would cozen and fatten their desired hog. It was all so impersonal these days. Especially with the damned phones as a factor. He had to resist the urge to snatch three such toys out of adolescent hands as he walked the streets, the little voyeurs seeing no issue with recording a stranger's face to moon over and share with the world at large. When he spotted a fourth phone, his willpower almost died to allow him to crumple both it and the fingers holding it to splinters. Right up until he realized the slab was aimed at another target.

The young man was quite oblivious, busy as he was with thumbing through a guidebook made thick with dogeared pages. Mason could see why his audience might stare. There was an appreciable balance between the handsome and the winsome in him that bordered near androgyny. Admirable height, tawny complexion, good architecture above and below the neck, and sooty lashes all combined to make a pleasing view. It was only damaged by the exhaustion in the eyes. Sleepless moons of dark brown paired with an even deeper russet in the irises that was nearly black.

All these observations came to Mason Darvell as secondary. He was temporarily stunned by the ravenous intake of another sense. One that almost obliterated the entire point of his visit in the surge of appetite that slammed through his veins.

The young man was absolutely *pungent* with goodwill. That and melancholy. Almost to the point of caricature. Whatever history existed for the boy prior to the sunny scene here, it was one in which good intentions had not only paved the way to Hell, but punched a hole straight down to the ninth circle where Lucifer sat waiting with open arms. There was a fissure running through the essence of him like a wound gone to rot with spiritual gangrene. He straightened and smiled whenever someone was approached for a question—answers apparently jotted in another volume, a plump traveler's journal—radiating all the ready cheer and utility of a dog.

Mason caught himself in a brief daydream of what his carotid artery would taste like. He pictured the dark eyes rolling and darting in that frantic confusion that always took them before expiration flooded out of heart and throat. He felt a nostalgic shiver as he thought back to the siblings in that long-ago London tryst. The ripeness of betrayal in their mirrored faces when the hour of epiphany came, the helpless rage of the boy and the rabbit-terror of the girl, seasoning the entire affair with that rarest euphoria in Mason's placid span of an unlife.

A twinkle of gold hinted at the source of the heady psychic whiff. It shined in a plain wedding band as the boy lifted a hand to rub his eyes. Eyes not merely tired, but sunken and solemn in the young face.

Loss. That's the core. Perhaps old. Perhaps new. Profound either way. Raw. Raw. Raw.

And, tantalizingly, as if the dish needed yet another garnish:
Alone.

It became obvious the instant the thought landed in him. If not by intuition, then by how the young man seemed in perpetual need of stopping short of embarrassment. Reaching to grasp a hand that wasn't there, head jerking up upon hearing the laugh or yelp of a child, turning to speak to a presence who didn't exist and quietly pinning his lips together again. If not a fresh robbery of domestic bliss, then an old one whose pain refused to be flattened by time's patient plodding.

The idea of divorce came and went like a breeze. There were some ex-spouses in the world who might shatter over such an ugly split, true. But Mason had a sense dedicated to that as well. He flattered himself to think it was one he had cultivated back in human days spent refining his pastime of the maimed psyche. He would swear he could smell the tang of funerals clinging to the young man like heavy cologne. Here was the ghost of turned earth, the odor of decay not quite masked under those white flowers which frothed from their vases and garlands...

The thought of flowers nettled him crudely out of the vision. Garlic. Rose. Ash.

Mason scowled to himself. How short a while ago would he have laughed at any hopeful fool brandishing the plants at him?

He'd once taken a wild rose for his boutonniere and used a crucifix to stab its quailing owner. And now—

Now the young man was leaving his bench and heading west. As he passed by Mason, his grey eye caught on the guidebook's page for St. Andrew's Church. Count Magnus' lair of the moment would be in the general vicinity. A bloated country home with a good view of the holy house and all its feeble pretense of protection. Mason wondered if the young man might try to flee toward it if Magnus set his pet on him.

Mason came up short in his shadowing. Only for a moment; the boy was as long-legged as himself and in better walking shoes. Yet he did pause.

If?

When. *When* Magnus called the familiar on him.

Though he admitted the thought now lost some luster. Any imbecile could serve the part regardless of how appetizing the soul's chemistry was. All that was required was the bastard's attention at an inopportune moment. And really, who was to say dangling new meat before the haughty old hermit was required? Especially when it was for a call that might be vital to both their continued existences. Hell, such an offering might be taken for a grovel. A *wasted* grovel.

"Pearls before swine," Mason murmured. He amused himself with throwing the whisper of it up to the young man's ear. This was followed by feigned interest in the horizon as his quarry jumped in skin now turning to gooseflesh. Mason felt the first wondering examination of the dark eyes on him.

"I'm sorry?" the boy got out. Mason turned to him with polite surprise. "Were you talking to me?"

"I didn't say anything," Mason assured. His eyes became hooks. The boy didn't move as he closed the distance. "Though I'd like to ask, were you heading toward St. Andrew's? I've been trying to play tourist and take the alleged scenic route but all I have to show for it is walking in a scenic circle. Which wouldn't be so terrible if I wasn't expected to turn up near there in," he brandished his phone for a glance at the time, "under an hour."

"Oh. Yes. Yeah, I'm heading that way, in theory." The young man brandished the guidebook. "I'm playing tourist too. Trying to fool myself into thinking I can put a travelogue together." The words struggled to carry a laugh. To cover this, he tucked guidebook and journal into the messenger bag at his hip and offered Mason a hand slightly spotty with graphite and ink. "Johan."

"Mason." He locked the warm palm in his hand's cold vise. "Are you mapping all of St Paul or just collecting churches?"

"Anyplace that seems worth wandering around and gawking at, really. We—," The word left Johan in the same heartbeat he realized the mistake. He swallowed it back as if he were eating a sewing needle. "I've always loved finding places to just loiter in. Wild spots and old places that aren't boxed in by," he pulled a face while gesturing at implied skyscrapers and advertisements, "everything."

Mason called on one of his reserve smiles, "If that's the case, the house I'm hunting for may be worth a look..."

Easy.

Always so easy once they were alone. Once they let him talk. Less a siren song than a steady suffocation of common sense. Not enough to render them lovestruck at a glance in the style of Miss Northcott's method, but enough to keep them magnetized. Welcoming. Blissfully oblivious to all the alarms ringing in the prison Mason built for them with a few heavy glances and soft patter. Better yet, this was aided by a pitifully pliant foundation in Johan Teller.

Mason had his theory proven right in quick fashion. Hearteningly, it was revealed while Johan struggled to hold his smile and strained to talk around the sharp debris of loss waiting for him at home. The expression almost creaked when he prattled about how travel had been a joint fantasy even when he and she were children. *Real* travel, mind, not just a trip to a popular venue or a crowded beach.

"We might squeeze in a theatre trip here and there, but we almost always wound up taking ourselves wherever it was open and quiet. A park, a cemetery. Places that weren't so choked. Though even that lost its shine for a while. We had a rather disturbing experience just before we got married. I was," his throat worked painfully, "I came down sick for a long while. My brain felt like it was boiling and the rest of me nearly fell apart. Some awful thing I picked up on a business trip. Not the best first mark for the thrills of visiting new places. She had to put me and my head back together for ages, it felt like. But that was just the one exception that proved the rule. The world was wider and better than one ugly example. And that stayed true for a bit. That little while we had with Arthur. We..."

But here Johan snagged himself as he had done on and off through their walk. His head shook as if the deep brown curtain of his hair might dismiss the memory the way a horse shooed flies.

"Sorry. I'm sorry, I don't mean to go on like that. I never used to just..." he flapped his hand at his mouth. "You've hardly gotten a word in and here I am giving a dirge." His voice splintered at the last word. He pointed to the church coming up to meet them.

"There it is now. I'll," he veered a few steps off toward the churchyard, "I'll just. Sorry."

He almost scuttled away, throwing desperate focus on fishing something from his bag so he had a reason to dip his head. The motion didn't quite hide the wet bead rolling down his cheek.

If Mason's stomach still functioned, it would have growled. In its place, his veins burned with such craving it made his teeth ache. The day's choice of dagger nearly sang in its pocket. His hand was already on Johan's shoulder. It stopped just short of crushing.

"*Don't.*" Johan peered up at him with a look wobbling somewhere between mortification, curiosity, and the first sharp prickle of worry. Mason scraped some of the ice off his tone and tried again. His hand remained where it was. "There's nothing wrong with," he nodded at the younger man's face, "this. If I'm being honest, I'd already guessed at it."

"What?"

"I don't know how to put it. Call it like recognizing like." Mason forced his grip to soften and his stare to go misty. "I can't begin to compare it to your loss and I won't pretend otherwise. But recently..."

Out of the ether came a heartbreaking rendering of the late Kate Northcott's death under grisly circumstances. A friend snuffed out of the world by her own fiancé. He had been due to march her down the aisle in place of an absent father. The wedding invitation was gathering dust in a drawer somewhere. He felt vertigo every time a pop-up ad appeared to flash tuxedos and wedding dresses in his face.

"Sometimes I'll go to call her, to take a photo of something absurd to annoy her with, and then it comes back. 'Oh. Wait.' Over and over. As if her being in a box in the dirt is just a fact that belongs somewhere else, to some other Kate. It can't apply to *her*. *She's* fine. She's always been fine. Untouchable. So," he almost choked, "so *in control* of everything. If she was going to die, it should have been something she set an appointment for. 'Yes, Death, meet you tonight in Samarra, don't be late.'"

Johan coughed up a laugh. A hoarse sound, teary, but real. His Kodak was fidgeted with, but, he'd grown no closer to the church.

"...I don't believe I've managed to mourn yet," Mason went on. "It's all just those little reminders. Being stabbed with the same pin I keep forgetting is there. I'll crack at some point. Maybe it'll happen in line for the cashier or on a walk or in the middle of dealing cards. Then," he snapped his fingers, "everything will strike home all at once. And I'll look like a blubbering idiot and Kate won't even be there to laugh about it. So. Do not apologize.

"All that said, I'll owe you a debt if you put off the church long enough to stop and look at Mag's house. Really, it's not a visit I'm entirely looking forward to, especially as it's a gamble on whether he's made a party of things. I'm quite allergic to his choice of guests." Here he put on his best plead. "If I have the excuse of a friend I'm traveling with who has places to go, so happy we could stop by, but we simply *must* be moving on...well. The rudeness scales will tip to our advantage. Mine, anyway."

Johan took a last steadying breath. Then the first glimpse of a genuine smile crept across his face.

"If that's the case, I don't think I'd have room to ask for a photoshoot of his place."

"You would. He'd be more offended if you weren't interested in it." As he spoke, he guided Johan back along the road, walking on, on, on until the air began to fuzz in a way that was not entirely visible to the eye. Not so much a heat haze as a greased spot in natural perception where the antique of an estate crouched, a place of technical charm and stealthy malignance. So it had been the last time Mason had seen it. The land had been a powerful locus stamped by Magnus' hand and so seemed to scowl or leer in accordance with his moods. Even the weeds had curled their lip at him.

Not so now.

"Oh," Johan breathed. New stars glinted in his eyes. He lifted the Kodak on reflex. "It's very fairy tale." It was true. In front of them was a grand old home lifted from a painted storybook. Birdsong crooned. Sunlight caught on the windows like cheery ponds. The stone gargoyles guarding the gate had gone from bloodthirsty to impish. A stray butterfly kissed the doorknocker. The rest of its cousins danced along verdant new growth in the yard.

Rosebushes.

Garlic blossoms.

Ash trees.

"Mason?" Johan's voice piped up from another planet. "What is it?"

He wasn't sure if he answered aloud or not. If he had, he hoped he hadn't spoken too much of the truth.

"Something's wrong," was as far as he could have gotten on that before he would have to add, "He was fine the last time I checked. He was *here*. Now he's nowhere." His head spun as he cast his senses as far as they could go, sniffing and searching for even a wisp of Magnus' presence trailing away. The only hint of him left was there. In the house.

It *could* be a trick. It *could* be a trap left for his uninvited associate to stumble into, the better to put on a show in a struggle with the familiar. It *could* be he was off on some spontaneous holiday away from his holiday. It *could* be.

Yet such ideas tasted too much like hope.

Said hope crumbled to atoms when he pushed open the gate and found the latch was not only undone, but in pieces. Johan followed after him, the Kodak forgotten after only a few cursory shots. He might have said Mason's name again. Then, louder:

"What's that smell?"

Mason didn't answer. He'd already noted the windows left cracked at the highest floor. The ones that would be set in the master bedroom. He tried the door. Unlocked rather than shattered. If he tried, he thought he could almost sketch the scene of it—the smashed gate reaching the old man's ear, the old man rising smugly up to unlock the door for his familiar to greet the uninvited guest, and then...

Suspicion bordering on premonition gnawed even as Mason tried to smother it.

Inside the house there was only a quiet gloom scarred by daylight punching through the windows. If Johan paled at the sight of Magnus' choice in interior décor, he either kept it to himself or else spoke in a whisper. Mason couldn't care either way.

"This isn't right, is it?" The young man asked in the tone of someone hoping to be proven wrong. "Maybe he's out?" But the back of his hand was pressed up against his nose. When Mason bothered to look back at him, he saw the unwanted revelation starting to sap the health out of his gaze.

"Stay down here."

"Wh—,"

Upstairs, something moved. Slithered. Possessed by the spirit of a suicidal Good Samaritan, Johan Teller moved toward the staircase. Mason took him by the arm and stopped just short of throwing him at the living room. Instead, he turned the boy to face him. The dead eyes were no longer hooks, but collars. Johan couldn't have looked away if he wanted to.

"You will stay down here until I come back. Promise me that. Right now."

The dark brow furrowed.

"I don't—,"

Mason Darvell laced every syllable with his will until they bristled with it. Unshakeable. Irremovable. Implacable.

"*Promise me.*"

"...Alright." Trying to blink some of the spell away, he managed to get out, "Should I call the police?" But Mason was already heading up the stairs. Regret was twisting in him before he reached the top.

The reek led him to the bedroom. Its door opened with an appropriately ponderous creak of the elderly hinges, though the effect was tainted somewhat by the abundant sunshine on the other side. There, spotlighted by a golden beam, was the resting place of Count Magnus. This was not hyperbole.

Sentiment had made the old man order the familiar to pluck his copper sarcophagus from its homeland and tote it wherever they traveled. The ornamented scenes in its ruddy shell were engraved reliefs of battles, executions, and even a respectable representation of the familiar itself at work. Such were all as Mason remembered them. But there were new copper shavings scattered on the hardwood that suggested an addition. Mason couldn't tell what it might be until he saw the lid was propped open on a broken padlock. More shavings dusted the exposed rim.

Mason counted to ten. Twenty. At thirty he felt Johan lay a tentative step on the bottom stair.

"*Remember your oath*," Mason willed down to his ear. He laid the suggestion of his cold hand on the boy's shoulder. Johan jumped as if goosed, whirling around once before retreating from the steps. The exertion was enough to shake Mason from his cobwebs. He reached for the lid.

The lid twitched.

Knowing the truth, not wanting to know, he had to ask, "Magnus?"

A half-remembered nightmare echoed back to him as an anathema's laughter gurgled from the black space inside the box. The owner of the sound coiled a limb up and out like a malformed snake. It lifted the lid gently up until Mason could see the full display.

The familiar had discarded the courtesy of its robe. A fact that nearly blinded him before the thing slithered out of the way and pooled wholly into the underside of the lid. Copper scraped and scratched beneath it as it worked. Mason gladly ignored this in favor of the second-worst view.

There hadn't been mercy enough in the creature to use its cloak to hide the results of Count Magnus' last social call. Whatever the man had done to himself while alive had altered his makeup to the point of eliminating the factors of human decay, resulting in his form of putrefaction melting into a far worse thing. A rainbow of the curdled, the dried, the liquefied, and the tumorous bulge-burst of strange innards had all rioted up from their foundation of bones and thrown a nauseating party around three wounds.

The first was a neatly stabbed gash where a heart once beat.

The second was the clean split between neck and shoulders.

The third was the raw and distinctly untidy removal of ninety percent of Count Magnus' face. Results of a very familiar sort of professional touch. Notably, there was more torn away at the eyes than anywhere else.

Mason bristled as the familiar slid itself out of the sarcophagus entirely, its coils lurching and piling until it was stacked up into the facsimile of a short human silhouette. Keeping only the barest corner of his eye on the thing, Mason lingered just a moment on the parting gift it had left engraved in the copper.

Here was a crisp depiction of Count Magnus' final moments. He was prone in profile, eyes bulging and hand raised in feeble shield. The artist had communicated the bewildered terror that had its attention split between both the hooded shape perched in a high corner of this very room and the looming character brandishing his great curved blade. The latter figure had no face beneath the brim of his hat. Only the hanging hair framing a shadow and the glint of eyes. In an almost delicate flourish, the artist had even wreathed the scene in a frame of particular blossoms.

Again that miserable laugh flowed like sewage to him. He dared a half-glance up. Just enough to see the fluid wretchedness of the maw. Somewhere in its murk, Mason thought he saw the spasming of a frail and diseased little light. It had an old man's wailing face.

I'll burn my books!—O Mephistopheles!

The maw sealed shut over the glow with a pleased gurgle. A limb rose in boneless salute. Then it was gone. Mason could only track the phantom of its departure and the bang of the door leading to the backyard which faced the woods. Johan punctuated the moment with a yelp. Followed by:

"Mason, can I—should I come up? Is something wrong?" He sounded near to gagging. Under his breath, "That smell's gotten worse."

Mason regarded the gruesome remains in their elaborate tub. Looking close, he saw something gleaming on the ragged stump of tongue remaining in the mouth.

A rough gold coin. Roman.

"Mason?"

Mason left the room on lead feet, thinking of bookcases, libraries, secret studies. None of which had helped the warlock in the end.

No. No, no, that wasn't fair. Any man would die from a snakebite if he didn't recognize it in time to treat his wound with the right antivenom. He didn't know Quinn Morse was coming for him. More importantly, his amorphous aide *had* known. Mason could almost envision the glee with which the familiar communicated, wordless yet distinct, the exact parameters of some old contract. 'Protection from the violence of mortal man,' or suchlike. Chores and slaughters on command, 'so long as you *live*.'

Yes. That was it, wasn't it? As long as he lived, albeit as a functioning dead man. And when Quinn Morse arrived to do what he did—

Ugly Hell, gape not!

Mason found Johan standing at the foot of the stairs, gawping up at him as he fidgeted with his phone. Deep doe eyes were now painted with flints of cognac by the changed angle of the sunlight. They would be art when the dagger slid home. Amber on fire...

Focus.

The house still needed searching for anything salvageable. Police would want a witness statement. Johan would slip out of his fingers and away from his teeth.

Now. He could do it now.

Or.

"False alarm," he sighed, being sure to crinkle his face in disgust. He moved down with a lazy hand in his pocket. It traced and retraced the jeweled pommel. "Couldn't tell you if it was the plumbing or something deciding to die in one of the walls, but I almost passed out up there. I wouldn't be surprised if he stepped out to avoid," another wrinkle of the nose, "all that. You haven't seen anyone down here, have you?"

"No, nobody. But I thought someth—someone might have gone out the back." Johan greened a little as he cast a look at the rear of the house. "I didn't see anyone out there but I thought I heard laughing. Maybe your friend went for a walk?"

"That or age is catching up to him. There's a fair chance he forgot our meetup was today. In fact, I'm sure of it now. I'm going at least as foggy as him to have missed the obvious."

"What do you mean?"

"His car is gone." Aided by the fact that said car didn't exist. "And considering the state of the place," he pressed at his nose, "I'm in no mood to hang around for him. We'll head out the back door. See if we can't save him a real burglary while he's out. I'll send him a head's up." Mason pulled out his own phone and began laboriously typing a text to no one. Johan took the hint and hustled off to lock the front door.

By the time they were back out on the road, the first fingers of evening were reaching up from the horizon. Johan snapped a handsome shot of this as the changing hues balanced like an illustrated backdrop to St. Andrew's.

"Apologies for wasting your time," Mason offered. "Likewise for the spoiled photo op."

"Not really spoiled. It's better in this light anyway." Johan snapped another shot. This one collected the weathered rows of some of the older headstones. "The only drawback is how brief this sort of light is. You get a blink of evening and then you can't even read the names. Though I guess some of these are too worn down for it to matter anyway. I can't even see half of this one. Anonymous Waxall or Wraxell or something."

Soon enough they were on their way back towards the little clot of civilization they'd begun in. Mason's hand drifted to Johan's shoulder.

"The least I owe you is a drink."

"Oh, I avoid the pubs. When I drink it's always too deep to hold myself together." Mason almost tried to wheedle with an assurance to see him to his hotel personally, but Johan flicked a cautious glance up through his lashes. "I only help myself in my room. Safer that way. I smuggled a merlot in rather than bother with the mini fridge." He swallowed. Doing so moved the lump of his throat with the same magic as a hypnotist's swinging watch. "If you promise not to tell on me to the staff, you can help me by removing a little temptation from the bottle. Shouldn't be trusted with the whole thing to myself anyway."

V

In time, Mason Darvell would learn that the hidden bottle was yet another plan intended for two rather than one. Something for mother and father while the boy was small, then to share when he'd grown. Johan Teller would apologize again upon mentioning this and try to pull his new friend to the metaphoric mic. Mason gave only fragments. Some invented, some merely repainted. He highlighted a certain holiday he had taken some while ago with another friend, a less recent loss to medical complication. An aneurysm of the brain took the young man's life not long after the two of them had returned to England.

"I like to think it was Providence lining things up that way. One happy tour to go out on before all the barbed parts of life could set in. Our last nights together were in the ruins of Italy and Greece. It was one of those few things we had in common. Craving the space and grandeur of those massive old masterpiece cities. Somehow we managed to hit a slow period between the tourist waves and we could pretend the world was just us and the faces we saw over the cards. Them and the girls." Mason composed a dreamy expression to reflect off the murk inside his glass. He had been faking a sip now and then, even allowing a few pointless drops past his lips. "The girls were nice," he half-mumbled, "and I think we did want them. Enough to love a little while. Enough to not think about each other in the next room."

Here he bit his tongue, shook his head, and set the glass aside. There was never blood enough in him to blush, but the sideways glance toward the bed did the work.

"This is why I'm hated by any and all bartenders. I make entirely too cheap a drunk. Give me grape juice and I forget why I know better than to talk too much." Mason slid an apologetic look to Johan still sunk in the opposite chair. A look made of hooks. "I understand if you'd prefer I left."

Johan neither stood nor leaned away. A half-emptied wineglass turned steadily between his hands.

"My wife's first kiss, and several more besides, were with her girlfriend. You are not the first man I've invited into a hotel room for a drink." He shrugged. "We both admired across the spectrum. So, no room to judge here." Johan lifted his glass as if in a toast. "I've already endured the worst-case scenario when it comes to discovering a new friend's preferences. Beyond the worst-case." His hand trembled just enough to make the wine ripple. He downed the rest of it in two neat gulps.

Mason didn't stop him from reaching for the bottle again, but faked another sip. The extrasensory perfume rising from Johan was so rich it dizzied. There was potent history rooted there. Deeply, intimately rooted. Mason pondered possible entertainment beyond dagger and fang as evening bruised into night. Talk burbled. Drink dwindled. At some point Johan murmured something about whether Mason had to go or not. Train? Car? Hotel?

Mason answered simply that he didn't have to go yet, no. Did he want him to?

Only if he wanted to, Johan hummed more than spoke.

The lamp made his eyes glitter a bleary ocher under the drooping lashes. One, two, three blinks later, the ocher was hidden in sleep. Mason plucked the latest glass from the lax hand and set it on the table.

For some long moments he regarded the dozing shape. The gift-wrapped ease of him. If Providence really was at work, then He had stacked the deck in favor of one of His usual cruel jokes. So it often went. Mason Darvell inhaled a deep mental breath and was hit again by the equivalent of a psychic buffet spread across a table of traumatized neuroses.

Yes, there had been a bad old friend once upon a time. A very close, very unwanted friend who had taken most extreme liberties. Him *and* friends of the friend if Mason had it right. Some manner of entrapment. A hostage to circumstances there was no wriggling or winning a way out of. Behave or else. Not blackmail, not even a Bluebeard routine, exactly, but *some* ugly ultimatum was in play. An employer? A landlord? Some coarser body in possession of a cellar that locked from the outside? Mason wondered and prodded but could find no definite form.

Something about appeasement hovered there. Tapdancing on a razor edge to the point of being willing to risk throwing his neck on that edge rather than go on that way forever. A narrow escape. Mason passed over that letdown of a relief and pawed back over the prior flavors as if trying to pinpoint every ingredient just from the scent of an immaculate dish. The echo-aroma of—

Let me go let me go want to go home please don't please no please no more

And then of—

No no no not happening must wake up we must wake up he didn't he couldn't have not this not to her no no no God why would You let this happen why did You let him happen

And—

Anything and everything for this for her for us anything and everything anything and everything I don't care I don't care anything everything for this for her for us forever

Mason only came back to himself when he felt the tickle of Johan's hair brushing his temple. An onlooker might have thought he was a man bowed to shove his face into a bouquet. Another of his kind might have shrugged and commented on his choice of fledgling. But Mason Darvell knew himself better and so came very near to carving Mr. Teller's heart out on the spot in retaliation to himself.

Adding more competition to hematophagous society was not now or ever on his list of priorities. The same went for having other suckling mouths to feed, no matter how handy an undead tagalong might be. It simply wasn't worth the headache. Now *this*. Mason brought out the dagger and let its point dimple the space between two of Johan's upper ribs.

No.

No, that wasn't right either. Was he to deprive himself of a prize over paranoia? Had he come so unglued?

He glowered at the blade and turned it so that fires danced in its garnets. There had been people at the desk. People in the streets who would recognize two men worth gawking at going off and up to this room together. And he *was* quite visible to security cameras, damn the things. An idle murder wasn't so easily fled anymore. Committing one here and now was imbecilic. Cowardly to the point of insult on top of that. Too jumpy, too distrustful of the original instinct.

But what *was* that instinct when stripped to its core?

Bite. Bleed. Turn.

Why?

The logical reason, once he sat with it, was obvious: he actually *could* use some competition about now. Rather, insulation. A palatable minion to order into the line of fire should the need arise. It was a sensible move at a comparatively negligible price. Fine. Understandable.

Yet 'fine' was not the full reason and he knew it. Just as he knew that so many others operated on new impulses once undeath set in. A hierarchy that was no longer one of needs so much as wants. Mason had always considered himself coolheaded, able to balance himself against urges too dangerous to act on in the moment.

But he'd just caught wind of an old abhorrence so powerful, so intrinsic to Johan Teller's mind, that the mere implication of it sparked nightmares despite years of padding between the present and whatever hell he had clawed his way out of. A loathsome dread of an ending that was no ending at all. Something to do with being bound to his dear old friend for keeps. No way out. No hope. No waking up.

Mason had never turned anyone before. Even if the whim had crossed his mind in this day and age, the world was positively bloated with fetishists and hopeful parties slavering to either join or grow their own ageless powerfully endowed undead harem. All the fear had been scoured out of them by romanticization so saccharine they had all but defanged the prospect of vampirism as anything but a gift. With a small fee, of course. Always to be paid by someone else. Donors or some nameless sheep there to sacrifice on the altar of their perfect prettily paranormal existence.

One of his last girls had been of that type. Stella. Their tryst had been a rare comical outing, him flashing his fangs and making a grand gothic show of how they were destined to rule the shadows as the world crumbled to dust at the feet of their eternal sensual love. He'd even asked her to pick out their first victims to break in their new unlife together and then fought not to laugh when she produced a list of enemies made in adolescent classrooms and assorted workplace annoyances. It had been worth it for her face when he slid the steel through her heart. The convulsions of confusion, epiphany, betrayal, and terror all shuddering through the last spasms of expression. It was as close as he'd ever come to experimenting with the concept. Once and never again, as baiting such game left a dull taste in his mouth once the entertainment value ended.

Not so with the promise lurking in Johan Teller's memory.

The potential of horror thrummed there—a horror of eternity, of servitude, of full and terrible understanding of possibilities worse than death. Mr. Teller had been prepared to die more than once in that muddy past rather than suffer whatever purgatory was thrust on him. All this being well before his grief over a family lost to the whims of natural cruelties. At the edges of it all Mason could trace the desire to be done with waiting and join wife and child in the afterlife. If he woke to a dagger slotted in his chest, there was little doubt that Johan would thank him for the courtesy.

And so Mason reconsidered the young man's throat.

Tomorrow? In a week or a month? He couldn't say. Not until after he had better ground to stand on with the Quinn Morse business. But the right time *would* come.

The first genuine smile of the night split his face. Ivory points gleamed in its borders.

"Do forgive me if I misstep in the future," he whispered into the sleeper's neck, "but you'll be my first." Supposing the thing called Quinn Morse didn't slice through the boy like screaming tissue paper, there could be entire centuries of learning opportunities ahead of them. Who knew? Perhaps he had been missing out all this time. He'd find out soon enough.

Though not tonight.

VI

All those of a bloodsucking bent could see at night. Some did so better than others.

Mason had always been relieved to find his own sight didn't obliterate the nightscape into the garish coloration of midday. Shadows still existed while the scenery chalked itself out in strokes of black and white, preserving the sensation of entering a more welcoming world. Few beautiful things moved him as much as meticulously orchestrated ugliness could, but the soft glory of nights away from the gaudy reach of metropolitan lighting was always an exception. Until recently.

Tonight he found himself glad of the car and the twin blasts of LED brilliance falling on the road. Even the presence of the sparse pedestrians that were his company heading back to his parking space had been shamefully comforting. Superstition had budded just enough in him to assume he might have better odds of survival among the potential innocent collateral. Failing that, he would still give the bastard as little an element of surprise as possible.

There were no surprises en route to Magnus' home. Nor were there any waiting to pounce as he left the vehicle. Moths fluttered. A dog barked somewhere. He went around the house while ogling every smudge of a shadow. All still, all clear.

Despite this, he found himself hating the groan of old wood as he nudged the back door open. He doubly hated how the floor creaked under his steps. There wasn't even a silver lining of more agreeable air to greet him. Magnus was still upstairs rotting away and sending out fresh clouds of stench to fill the building. Mason gave a brief thanks that his breathing was purely optional and promptly opted out of it as he hunted. Minutes fattened into more than an hour as he scanned room after room for anything more illuminating than the dead warlock's taste in occult bric-a-brac. None of it was even passingly imbued with magic. Only artfully rendered agonies and evils that could double as décor.

The books were wastes on top of that. Here were fictions and history texts all cluttered with annotations that either insulted or lauded the writers' attempts at barbarism on paper. There wasn't even the hope of a hidden room or subcellar here. The house itself was the secret, guarded as it was from mundane senses. Yet the place was wholly bereft of useful arcana. It looked as if the man had squatted happily on his old arcane winnings since acquiring his familiar.

Had he burned his worthwhile books? Had there even been any to burn? Mason almost dared to suck in a rancid breath to curse.

He checked every corner, every closet, every inch of floor, wall, and ceiling for a discreet panel or partition that might bear fruit, and found nothing.

Apart from one spot.

Redoubling his resolve against inhalation, the last stop was made in Count Magnus' bedroom. The sarcophagus still sat open to proudly exhibit its contents. He regarded the soup of profaned flesh and disintegrating bone. It was the only evidence the old bastard had left behind that suggested acquaintance with the infernal. Whatever secret intel he might have had was now towed down to Hell with its squealing owner.

Mason was about to slam the lid shut when a thought occurred to him. It was almost as heartening as it was disgusting. The sarcophagus *was* old. As old as the man's first death. The copper vessel was the same one he was entombed with, the same one that had traveled from his family crypt to each new roost. His one constant piece of luggage, guarded the closest out of any property by him and his hireling horror. Meaning...

He mouthed airless profanities.

Rather than reach directly into the bodily slush, he opted to tip the sarcophagus up on its edge. Mason boosted it easily and kept his head canted away from the mess as the copper gave up its tenant. There was a horrendous slosh and clatter of decay spilling onto the hardwood. This was capped with a far less organic sound. A sodden papery flutter with a damp little *thump*. Mason lurched the oblong weight away with a shove and crouched over his prizes.

The first thing to catch his attention was a small slab wrapped in leather and secured with elaborate cording. Miraculously, it had been spared from the worst of Count Magnus' dissolved muck by dint of the hide. The cargo within had not one stain on it. A slim old pocket notebook bound in soft calfskin, its pages thin and yellowed by time. Mason thumbed through a few leaves carefully. A good deal of enthusiasm dimmed when he saw there was not a word of any intelligible language written inside. But there *was* writing.

Mason frowned over the strange dashes and squiggles packed edge to edge on every leaf. It had to be a cipher. There was no key tucked anywhere that he could see, but it was a start. It went to his pocket. His attention then turned to the consolation prize scattered like square leaves amid the mess. He flipped one over.

Recognition made him first slow, then freeze. Gradually he thawed enough to turn over as many as he could without dipping his fingers in the fetid remains.

Photographs. Kodak shots. Not like the digital images sealed away in Johan's little toy, but the monochrome offerings of the box models passed around toward the far end of the 19th century. In each photo there was a headstone. Two of the oldest sported the weathered markers of two Swedes. One of the English stones had been seen in person that very evening.

Impulse betrayed him enough to suck in a small rotten gasp. It was then that he noticed something new cutting through the room's odor.

Roses. Garlic. Ash.

In the same mistaken breath, he took note of the broken moonlight now falling against the floor. Broken, because something tall obstructed the white glow of the window behind him. It wore a broad-brimmed hat. An arm lifted something curved high overhead.

Mason lunged away as the air split where he'd been crouching. He felt the loss of a lock of hair at the back of his head while his coat and shirt gained a slit between the shoulder blades. Gooseflesh leapt up along his spine. Reflex had already whirled him around and unsheathed his own blade. The impulse withered to dust when his eyes met *its*.

'His' eyes, ostensibly. It had surely begun as a man. Even obliterated as the face was by the backlighting of the moon and the shadow of the brim, the body and attire *were* human. At least as human as Mason. But the eyes could not support the lie. Even in the void behind the spider silk hair, those eyes burned hollow and bright.

It would be polite to liken them to stars.

It would be honest to admit they were the clouded shine of a corpse's stare. Or else the coins laid on them in the box.

Cold flowed from them. The kind that belonged to the vacuum of space, to cessation itself. For one nauseous instant Mason was shunted back half a millennium into the sweating meat and marrow of a man riddled with sickness. A man who felt the failure of his body, so long an ally in the lucrative and pleasurable harvesting of lives, betraying him at his prime with faulty construction. How he had shuddered then, bleeding, reading, begging, bargaining to the god-thing with her triad of faces, clambering away from the pit of death and the damnation at the bottom of its merciless well on hands and knees.

That pit was here now. Looking through him.

The curved blade raised again—a nattering voice in him announced that it was of handsome make, smithed and whetted so finely it might shave the wings from a fly without it noticing—and swung for him. It was a far closer miss. Not even a whole dodge, for the tip of the steel sliced a neat line through the thick part of his shoulder. Cloth and skin unzipped in a way that went beyond the simple throb of bullets and gashes he'd shrugged off before. A crumbling numbness was flowering there, and with it came a horrid, stinking softness. Shudders ran down his arm and nearly made him drop the dagger as his fingers tried to go limp.

He thought of the last moments of Kate Northcott drying to desiccation on camera. He thought of the malformed puddle of Count Magnus at his feet.

No.

No.

Quinn Morse surged forward. Mason darted around him, fleeing to the further window. Still open.

He flung himself out and through the gap, first catching himself on the boughs of an ash tree with a wince and then hopping to the ground. The direct fall of moonlight was an instant balm. As was the nearness of the car. The keys came out, Mason got in, and the tires squealed as they backed away to the road. But as he turned the wheel with his good arm, a strange thing happened.

Something took flight out of the bedroom window. It shattered the pane in its clumsy exit and blocked the moon as it soared. Mason almost took it for Mr. Morse himself until he recognized the shape of the projectile. An oblong thing that shined with copper.

Magnus' sarcophagus punched squarely into the nose of the vehicle, crunching metal and sending an explosion of cracks along the windshield in a deafening landing. Steel crumpled like foil and the revving heart of the engine died. Mason scrambled from the seat just in time to see something else leaving the window. Not another dramatic flight, thankfully, but one that filled his bowels with ice just the same.

Quinn Morse was climbing out. Scaling his way down the wall with the ease of a colossal spider. The head swiveled to look at him. Even at this distance, the dead eyes blazed in their shadow of a face.

Only three options occurred to Mason Darvell as he began the night's long run for his unlife. He could hide alone, he could hide with people, or he could go on running and hope his pursuer gave up the chase. After running on the road, through the woods, across a cemetery, and through a frustrating abundance of dark and sleepy little houses without losing his new companion, the last option was abandoned. There wasn't even enough of a pause to consider breaking into a building or ducking out of view. Quinn Morse was a singularly determined hunting dog who kept a constant line of sight and a pace to match Mason's own.

Always a match, Mason noted with a bitter realization. He wasn't being hunted so much as herded. This was all but confirmed when it finally occurred to him to fish out his phone. He managed to make it to the dialing screen before a shot fired and a bullet blasted the fragile wafer out of his hand in a spray of plastic.

Whatever Quinn Morse was, he was not lacking for armory, aim, or speed. The chase was only going on because he wished it to. Playing with his food. How long had Miss Northcott had him as a beau? How long had he been circling Magnus? How much time was left for him?

Enough to last the night, as it turned out.

He learned this when a misplaced step in a pothole nearly flung him into the asphalt. It forced him to stumble and twist just enough to notice he appeared to be alone. Either satisfaction or the artificial glow of civilization had steered Mr. Morse away from the race. Mason made the rest of his trek without blinking or pausing. With car and phone and an entire arm out of the picture, there was only one option he considered even partway feasible. But there was work to do first.

He was sickened but not surprised at what he found when he shrugged free of his sleeve. A blossom of necrotizing black rot unfurled over the high part of his shoulder. The bullet he'd taken in Rome had gone just as bad, but only after days of waiting. Just another caveat of his status. Wounds weren't so cheaply hidden or healed as with other variants; they showed the dead flesh for what it was under the unnatural health. Had this been an ordinary case, he might have been content to let himself sleep down to death and lay himself out on a rooftop to soak up the moon and replenish himself. But he could take no chances now.

Not when that torpor might end with him decaying down to nothing mid-drowse. Quinn Morse could be lurking and waiting for that very moment. Sharpening his blade as Mason settled down to rest and ignore the wound away.

There was no choice.

Mason Darvell set the dagger's ornate sheath between his teeth and bit it in lieu of a wooden block. The dagger itself was gripped in his good hand. He counted to ten, then went to work while the moon watched.

VII

Mason could hear a shower running when he pressed his ear to the door. A few loud knocks later the spray stopped. There was a fuzzy murmur of either confusion or complaint.

"Johan," he said through the door. The murmur stopped. "Can you help me with something?" The door clunked its heavy bolt and swung in on the sight of a sodden Mr. Teller in a bathrobe. Upon seeing his returned guest, Mr. Teller's eyes ballooned until they almost fell from his skull. This was to be expected. Mason had made sure to shuck the covering of his ruined shoulder for maximum effect once he got past the front desk.

A tidy notch of flesh had been sawed out of the muscle, leaving no traces of rot behind. None of Quinn Morse's rot, anyway. A wound was still a wound and it would start to decay again in a few days' time. He'd still need his moonlit routine. But there was time now. At least enough to ensure other matters were taken care of.

"What happened?" was the first thing out of Johan's mouth as he guided Mason in by his good arm, eyes dancing back toward the hall as if some lunatic with an axe meant to follow him inside. He locked the door after them. "Mason, talk to me, what is this? Do we need the police or the hospital first?"

"Neither. Do you have a medical kit?" Even as he asked, Johan was coming back with a roll of gauze taken from a box under the sink. Quick fingers went to work cleaning and wrapping.

"This isn't going to be good enough. You'll need stitches."

"No."

"Just let me get dressed—,"

"No."

"—I think I saw an all-night cl—,"

Mason's good hand flew and caught Johan's wrist just as it lifted his phone.

"*No.*" Johan gawped warily at him. Straining, Mason sketched a pleading look over his glare. "Please. I'm not sure how safe we'd be." His grip lightened. "I can't risk anyone assuming things, seeing you with me."

Over the next hour Mason pieced together a feasibly frightful outline of events involving a late-night walk to find his car again. How he'd thought nothing of it until the attack. Someone he recognized had driven the knife through him. Someone he knew from experience the police would be no help with. The car, he'd discovered just prior to being jumped, had been rendered useless. Everything that could be destroyed by an industrious hand had been. Even the ignition was cut. His phone was lost in the scuffle. Ironically, he was left with his wallet. Hate trumped petty theft, it seemed. No, no hospital, no police. None here, anyway.

"The silver lining is that he may think I've moved here rather than just stopping by. If I can get back home unnoticed, he can go on thinking so."

"You're being stalked," Johan said with a hand kneading his brow. He spoke mainly to the window whose curtains he kept peeking through. Once more seeing nothing worth noting, he turned to face Mason in full. "I imagine it's hard to miss someone dressed like a gothic Victorian cowboy while he runs around stabbing people and vandalizing cars. The police could at least put a warning out, have someone drive by your place once you get home. Something's better than nothing."

Mason summoned his weariest smile and let the falseness of it shine through.

"I've only had my new house for a month. Three guesses as to why I moved from the last one." Johan dragged both hands down his face. "Exactly."

"That's insane. All of this is insane." The young man shook his head, now looking a decade older. "Is this a hitman you're dealing with? A," he gestured feebly, "a professional or something?"

"I don't know. I've made people quite upset in the past. Romances that made certain third parties less than happy with me, even when those relationships broke off."

"Any names come to mind?"

Mason shrugged specifically to wince and sighed, "Too many possibilities. Part of the excuse the police keep on hand for why this is still happening. But I'm tired of talking about it tonight." He peered at the creeping dawn coming through the curtains. "Or today. I know this is asking too much already, hiding up here while my friend is sniffing around. Though daylight should be safe enough. Too much visibility for him. I can probably make it to the train station..."

The effect was immediate to the point of seeming autonomic. There was no sudden tide of goodwill coming from Johan Teller that Mason could detect so much as a switching of gears. Within the hour they were on the road. Whatever thin protestations Mason made as to his driver's own holiday and travel plans were swept away. A home address was wheedled from him just before Mason found himself bundled into the backseat of Mr. Teller's car, blanketed and pillowed. No, he would not be paying to fill the tank. Go to sleep.

It was noon by the time they pulled up to Mason's latest lodging. Johan had hesitated due to the overgrown yard. He swallowed a line about Mason being a bit too out of sorts to bother with the upkeep of the place for the last month. Or even moving the bulk of his things in. Not in the proper headspace and all that. His visit with his old ex-professor was intended to be his first act of interaction with anyone beyond food delivery in some while.

"Then you happened." Shrug, wince. "Silver lining." His good hand found Johan's shoulder while the other cradled his housekey. "Thank you for doing this."

"I wouldn't have lived as long as I have without strangers willing to believe me in strange circumstances. Even some who didn't." A shell of mingled memories hovered around him. Old fear, old gratitude, old anger. "You have to pay that kind of thing forward. Is there anything else I can do?"

"Yes." Mason hooked him by the eyes. "Promise me you'll come by again in," he groped for the lunar cycle's shape, "a week. Just to make sure I'm not dead. And to repay the drink." Concern floundered in Johan's face. It hardened as Mason gave his shoulder a squeeze too near to his neck. "Please. *Promise me that.*"

"I promise." The words seemed to trudge out of Johan's lips, but once they hit the air they became fact. Blinking the ensuing internal fog away and stifling a yawn, he added, "I can turn up sooner if you need it. My place isn't too far from here." A new yawn rose to slip past his hand. "Won't even need to bother finding a room."

"If you can forgive the mess on one side and the haunted house sparseness on the other," Mason unlocked the door, "you're welcome to nod off here."

There was a brief demurral before Johan found himself herded in. Mason watched him take in the nakedness of the house. Unlovely but for the damask drapes choking out the noontime sun. Despite this, there was no whiff of surprise from the boy. In its place was recognition. Mason wondered what manner of home was waiting for the young man upon his return. A barren box that used to hold life and love and now just held dust. The sensation was shuffled away as Mason corralled him toward the master bedroom.

All his materials had been shut away in their safe before Mason had left. The bed sat made and waiting at the room's center.

"I won't be sleeping," he informed his guest, perhaps an inch too close to his ear. "And there's no couch to dump you on anyway. So." He gestured at the broad spread of the bed. Plush with covers and comforters all plump with fine fillings and swaddling texture, all with the smallest hint of claret in the myriad fabrics. Mason watched from the corner of his eye as Johan stared down at it. He pressed an unsteady hand into the thick top cover until his fingers sank in it like snow.

More memory. More echoes of nausea and dread long past. How young must he have been for it to be such an old wound? How old was he now? Depending on the moment Mason could have pinned him as a boy fresh from high school or a man scraping the beginning of his thirties.

Now, inexplicably, he appeared to be both. The frightened child and the adult mourning him.

"Is something wrong?" Mason ventured. He had shed his coat and kicked off his shoes. The pocket journal was already hidden in a trouser pocket. He worked idly on the shirt buttons. Johan glanced up at him, saw his progress, and looked sheepishly away. He pulled his hand back from the bed and rubbed at his wedding ring as if soothing an animal.

"No. Yes. I just—I don't want to impose—,"

"You won't." The shirt was gone. Its torn shoulder smiled up at him like a stained mouth. He made slow work of pawing around in his wardrobe. "I'll play the victim card if I must. Also the 'you're bloodshot as a tomato and will drive into a tree if you don't rest' card." He selected a shirt and turned back to face Johan. Johan was studying his shoes. "If you're worried about anything from my end, don't be. I'm in no shape to pounce." He waited for Johan to look up before he grinned. He made sure to show his teeth. "We'd have to wait a week for that."

Johan Teller didn't budge. Nor did he blink. There was a tired huff in place of a laugh. Whether he took it for a joke or a genuine segue was a mystery.

"I guess we'll see." So saying, he laid himself on the covers. His eyes shut against the view of his host. "Wake me if your killer cowboy shows up." And that was that.

Mason took himself out of the room for half an hour before peeking back in again. Johan Teller had not moved. In fact, he was still to the point that another observer might have worried. Yet his heart still beat and his skin was warm to the touch. A fact Mason made sure to double-check. Throat. Wrist. Chest. Cheek. Mr. Teller slept through it all like a stone. If he didn't, then his heartrate betrayed nothing. Nor did his dreaming. Love and despair pulsed dully in the latter.

"I could do anything right now," he whispered to the sleeping face. "Anything. And you would still come back in a week. Do you know that?" Johan neither agreed nor disagreed. "It's true." He smiled. Coiled a dark brown lock around one finger. "I wonder how you would rationalize it. It's always been one of the better parts of the game. The oaths they were always so shocked to find themselves keeping. So few people watch their words anymore. They see no weight in things like idle promises. It's such a treat to see the moment they realize there's no breaking it. No lying their way through what was given as truth. They said they would, so they must. No helping it."

Faces fluttered past in a parade of broken minds and helpless mental bowing to a hundred thoughtless oaths. He imagined Johan's among them, twisted in uncomprehending shock as he marched himself back through the door and into Mason's hands despite...

Despite what?

His hand rested on the warm throat without daring to press. No more than he dared to peel the sleeper's clothes and idle through the vulgar mechanics of assault. Why not? *Why not*?

"You are nothing special." His breath broke against Johan's cheek. "You are a distraction barely a day old. Time might tell otherwise. But I doubt it." He tasted the lie as it left him. There was no doubt. There was no weight at all in his tongue. Searching, he still found no reason for it. In that unreasonableness, he found an urge to rattle the boy awake to appreciate his situation—supposing he would care.

Why did *he* care?

He tore himself from the bed before he could go digging for another answer he wouldn't find. There were more pressing concerns. One of which was still waiting in his pocket. In a locked room he thumbed carefully through the fragile leaves, comparing the cipher there to the glyphs and dead tongues stamped across sundry volumes of diablerie. That he could find nothing comparable to the meaningless scratching was made all the more infuriating by the fact of its familiarity. He had seen something like it somewhere before, he knew it, but the meaning of the aimless jots and squiggles was absent.

One of many casualties a mind faced after going on so long. The answer had fallen into the same bottomless well where his birthday and the names of his blighted parents had dropped ages ago.

"You hardly had any worthy spies, you miserable bastard," he groused to the mocking pages. "Why bother?"

A small knock made him jump. He went to the door and found Johan waiting on the other side, flipping through his own journal. It was a sturdy thing gone half-black with scribbling and made considerably thicker with its use as a scrapbook. Newsprint, postcards, brochure clippings and photographs bloated the thing. Johan clapped it shut as Mason opened the door.

"Hey. Just wanted you to know I'm heading out. Left my number on the nightstand if you need it." He seemed about to continue when his gaze fell to Mason's hand. The last threads of sleep left his eyes. Excitement wafted from him in waves. "You write shorthand too?"

Mason looked down and saw he hadn't released the journal. His thumb was pressed as gently into the first page as he could manage despite his desire to rip the thing into confetti. Seeing it now, he realized Johan had hit upon it—it *was* shorthand. Though he'd never learned the styles himself, hazy recollections of the typewriter's infant days now came back to him. With them came the memory of the odd bustling journalist or typist's hasty pen jotting down gibberish.

Before Mason could invent a reply, Johan had turned his own volume around to display its latest entry. Here were more nonsensical scribbles, albeit in a different style.

"I do Teeline. Yours looks like...oh wow, I haven't seen Pitman in forever. Is it for a project or just for fun?"

"Neither," Mason managed to say evenly. "It isn't my writing. Just some old thing I found in a sale." He turned it gingerly in his hand, holding the pages out. "...You can read this?"

Johan frowned at it a moment, humming, "Only bits and pieces. There's something about Munich, somebody traveling. I'd need to sit down with a reference before I could get anything solid out of it. If you like, I could borrow it and bring it and translations back once I've got it all down." He reached for the little book before stopping short. "Unless you'd rather I not. It looks antique."

"It is. I would rather hold onto it." The hooks returned to his eyes. Then, before he knew he was saying it, "Can you get your reference material from your place?"

"Would you like me to play tutor?"

"I'd rather pay a translator fee." Another unpleasant spark flew up from Johan Teller's mind. An ugly little flare tinged with thoughts of a Fly beckoned into a Spider's parlor on business. *There's a job to do, friend. Please do stay awhile.* "Or we could change location. You can come here or I can come to you. Assuming you'd feel safe, considering..."

"I'm fine either way." Johan almost crushed his own journal as he said so. He stroked the wedding band again and again. Mason beamed at him.

"Come back in a week, then." He held up the slim journal. "For me and this. Hopefully things will look a bit more livable by then."

VIII

Johan Teller went away and the week went with it. As did death and the moon, both erasing the cold rawness of his mangled shoulder. He masked the impossible new flesh with a sizable plaster before setting to the menial labors of turning the house into something simultaneously sumptuous and unpalatable. The latter was taken from a fine hint he'd tasted as Johan went out the door. The bareness of the walls had been disquieting. But the furnished bedroom, to say nothing of the bed itself, had plucked far more unpleasantly at old wounds.

It had been a lavish backdrop where those nameless intimate violations happened. A regal demesne, all dark decadence and bodice ripper daydreams. Or so it might have been for another, thumbing through pages of pulp and escapist twaddle. Johan Teller had lived it to some degree. Even the presence of velvet fired hateful reminiscence through body and brain.

All of which encouraged Mason Darvell to treat himself. One eye was reserved for the nights, wary should Mr. Morse make himself known, while the other eye was spared to harass 24-hour delivery services into making them sprint for every cent he dropped on swamping the walls with oppressive splendor. Tarnished gold, glints of burgundy amid the black, grotesquerie disguised as opulence. He even hung up his blades, arranged a cardroom, and added food to the kitchen.

Between preparation and paranoia, he found time to go over the books again. There was nothing new to glean from what was already read beyond the usual 'it could bes.' It could be a familiar hired out as an assassin to the undead. It could be an embittered dealmaker out for revenge with power from the divine or the diabolic to dispose of them. It could be one of those dreary self-loathing sorts made undead against his will exercising his grudge on a wide scale, likewise empowered by Higher or Lower Powers That Be to make sure even the impervious barterers could be put in the grave. Could be, could be, could be.

Whatever Quinn Morse was, he or some backer had haggled to gain his edge.

Which implied that *somebody* on the other side of the deific fence was sick enough of the revenant brigade that they were willing to part with an extra dose of power to outweigh everyone else's death-defying contracts. Who did that suggest? The gods and devils responsible for the pacts, all suddenly wanting to collect their due at once? Had the opposing seraphic sorts finally ended their celestial smoke breaks en masse to bless some lone lunatic with a holy crusade? Whoever was responsible, why had they chosen to send their dog in *now*?

He groused over the tomes at his left and the cookbook at his right. Intuition had nettled him again to announce that, paradoxically, even the gesture of having a meal prepared when Johan walked in the door would key certain ugly memories. There had been a sensory impression of tastes that would always carry a bitter recall for the young man. Roast chicken and Tokaji were prominent flavors. The oven went to work on the bird as he toyed with the stem of a wineglass and tried not to break it.

It was as he was thumbing through one of his own ledgers that he thought back on the first death of note. The boyar.

Count. Warlord. Prince. Alchemist. Sorcerer. Whatever else he had been in life and unlife, he was one of the most powerful of their lot well before he sunk himself in an upgraded iteration of vampirism. Paired with all the mystic tricks he'd possessed as a man, his strength and resistance to countering powers had been swollen to excess. Hence his remaining idle and satisfied among the terrified Christian chattel in the mountains while still managing to drink them thin to the point of having to change hunting grounds. So Mason had assumed.

The would-be conqueror had moved from the Carpathians to the crowded streets of England over the course of a summer. Then, for reasons unknown, he'd rushed straight back to his mountains by mid-autumn. Mason had sensed it the way one might hear the loping of some ponderous animal skulking one direction and then sprinting back the other. Leisure versus a rush. That had been in 1893. Back and forth across the Channel within the space of two seasons, and then *poof.* Gone. The ensuing years had proven his absence by how the joyous locals had stripped his estate bare before the end of the decade. But 1893 was what mattered. The true start of it.

Something had happened to make him run. Something he'd found waiting in England which had gone tearing after him all the way home. Whose toes could he have stepped on here? Of such parties, who among them would have the knowledge and ability to call on something powerful enough to deliver a permanent ending rather than the nuisance of temporary demise? All the truest texts and rites of bygone ages had been hoarded away by the eldest of their kind.

A successful practitioner didn't just leave secrets like that laying around for any piddling Wiccan or devil worshipper to paw at. What couldn't be hoarded was destroyed and what couldn't be destroyed was buried. Although England was a notorious thieving magpie of a country, he knew none of its museums or libraries had snapped up anything of real use.

Which opened new questions in itself. Whoever had conjured or converted Quinn Morse back then, how exactly had it been pulled off? What could be offered that would be worth the power he had?

The oven dinged and Mason shook the thought away. It was all moot until he had a foundation to work with. There had to be some clue hidden in the damning trip to London just as there had to be some secret to Quinn Morse's current hesitation. Leaving him to run and rot when it was so obvious that—

"He could have made it quick," he informed the set table. As an afterthought, he brought out candles. "The villages were wiped out too fast for him to have let things dawdle. Why let it linger for us?"

Johan Teller's dinner had no answer for him. This was just as well, for the doorbell rang a minute later. Johan seemed pleased to find Mason alive and markedly less pleased to find the surprise of the meal. Doubly so when Mason declined to eat himself, claiming some doctorial order kept him from solids. Drinks and supplements had been and gone. Help yourself.

The hours moved like silk over Mason's senses as he inhaled the mingled tides of Johan's unease bordering on sickness over the new trappings. Mason thought the boy was near to leaping out a window when the inevitable invitation to stay the night was made. Instead, he heaved a small sigh through his nose.

"This is too soon for me. I know it shouldn't be. It's been years since," his throat worked, "since all of it. Part of me thinks I could go on a thousand years and it would still be too soon for me to ever picture trying again. Plus," his hand laid itself gently over Mason's, "I can't help thinking you're pushing yourself into this."

"Me?"

"You. You've been stuck in a dangerous position on top of a very recent loss. If you're not scared, then it feels like you're reaching for—I don't know. Closeness. A distraction. Something that makes more sense than trying to pull this kind of intimacy out of nowhere after barely two days' acquaintance."

"I'm rarely sensible when it comes to things like this," Mason rebutted. His hand maneuvered until it lay on top of Johan's and squeezed. Another blissful gust of discomfort was knocked loose. "It's one of a few things that get me into trouble in the first place."

"I won't be part of that trouble, then. Not in the way you want. If you're short a friend," Johan's foot nudged the messenger bag against his chair, "or a translator of outdated chicken scratch, I'm happy to oblige. But I can't give more than that to anyone I don't love. I have loved exactly once in my life." His gaze was glass. "My heart went into the dirt with her."

Mason imagined the slide of steel going through his chest.

No, it's still right where the sow left it. See?

He ran his thumb over Johan's knuckles.

"I didn't intend to push too hard. If I'm being honest, I'm a bit embarrassed at myself. I'm acting like the sort of idiots Kate and I used to laugh at. The kind who trip over their own feet once they think..." Mason shook his head. "I don't think I have the right words. I just know I've felt more comfortable since knowing you than I have in months. Maybe years. Which makes no sense even if it is the truth. Even if it's selfish on top of stupid to have crossed my fingers for something more so soon, considering the current admirer trying to sniff me out."

"It's not stupid," Johan murmured. His hand shifted against the iron grip Mason had it in, just enough so that they were intertwined. "And it's not selfish. It's just human. My friends and I lost someone dear to us a while back. Most of said friends had a crush. One was due to marry her. Then," he waved his free hand, "she was gone. Just like that. Died in bed. And the loss, sick as it seems in hindsight, locked us all into this kind of grief-bound love. We were lucky to have each other for support, but the pain galvanized it into something that probably wouldn't have come naturally otherwise. We'd only been in each other's circle less than a month. But there we were. Together for life. Some of us getting less of the latter than they were due, of course." Johan tried to chuckle and it came out like a choke. "See? Red flag for you right there, if you need one. I keep outliving people I care about."

"Then it's only right, isn't it?" Mason countered. "Someone else has already beat you to the impending doom threat." He caked on some solemnity of his own. "If something does end up happening, I'd rather it be with a memory of better company than his. Whatever company you're willing to give."

A melancholy so deep it became a chasm seemed to open up in the boy. The kind that had greased sides impossible to climb and which begged for bullets and opened veins, for explosive lightning bolts and lengths of knotted rope. It was a misery that had ceased considering death as anything but a tantalizing alternative compared to the sluggish march of life.

Mason was almost embarrassed at how his teeth ached over the thought of taking the option away. He had to hold his fangs in with a purposeful flinch. Thoughts of juveniles shamefacedly crossing their legs came to mind. Johan stared at their locked hands, oblivious.

"I'm tired of losing things, Mason. I've lost people. I've lost joy. It feels like I keep finding and misplacing my sanity. This," he held up their hands, "feels too much like the start of another loss."

"And nothing else?"

Another flash. Bitter, weeping, screaming memories before a vulpine smile.

"Nothing worth mentioning. I'm sorry if I led you to believe I was looking for—for anything like this. But I can't do it."

"I can."

Johan bristled as Mason's other hand found his jaw and forced him to look up. Memory again. Cold hands making themselves at home on him, never invited. The silence that came like a reflex. Neither flight nor fight, but a freeze.

Be quiet. Be good. Be patient. It will hurt less.

Mason thumbed Johan's cheek and traced a line there.

"You strike me as the type of person who accommodates everyone but himself. The good, the bad, the giving, the selfish. If it makes them happy, you bow to their needs first. Once you're alone, you have only yourself to consider and so you don't bother. Am I wrong?" Johan didn't answer, but tried to hide the death grip he now had on his armrest. The hand in Mason's own was limp. "Would you stop me if I kissed you? Would you tell me outright not to do it?"

"I'd prefer you didn't."

"Doesn't answer the question. Would you tell me *no*? I ask, because I know I'm selfish. And I am drunk and dense enough right now," so he could pass as, having swished and spat several mouthfuls of wine into the sink before answering the door, "to act like it." Mason closed the space between them to a meager gap. Johan leaned away as far as the chair would allow, but did not stand. Quiet. Good. Patient. *Over soon, my friend, you are doing so well.* "Tell me no, if you want." If he could.

Johan was silent. Which was fine. Mason could taste everything clearly enough.

The night was long.

The night was a blink.

The night reeked of candle wax and skin.

The night brought Mason to an edge he hadn't known existed, a temptation wholly alien and mesmerizing as Johan lay below, sunk in grudging pleasure and the aftershocks of bygone suffering. Not for the first time, Mason wished it was as easy to take succor from the sensation as from blood. Blood which still pumped on and on in unbroken living veins. Mason's fangs seemed prepared to pierce straight through his own lip to get on with the full consummation, but he held them back with every kiss, every taste. He was relishing the preliminary performance for the first time in...

Had it really been since the smitten little English lordling and his sister? Yes, he thought so. Only Johan Teller was a hundred times headier. Even in sleep, the young man magnetized. Mason thought dreamily of Fuseli's painting and how fixed the Nightmare had looked while perching on the dreaming woman's breast. What had that creature been thinking of to look so displeased with its prey? Mason thought he knew now.

Perfect. Here was a feast made entrancingly *perfect* for consumption, for conversion into a supple payoff. But once the feast was had, it could never be eaten the same way again. The human horror died for the undead self to exist. Johan Teller would remain sane as a vampyre of Mason's variety. Aware of all that had been stripped from him in being forced to choke down eternity and fealty. And it *would* be a delightful show as the epiphany sank in. But Johan Teller the Human would cease to exist and tease the palate just the same.

So Mason Darvell loomed. Waited. Watched.

Starved.

...How long *had* it been since his last drink?

He left Johan still twisting in his unhappy dreams just as night turned late enough to skirt the morning. Mason slunk out of the house with visions of dark alleys and broken windows dancing in his mind.

Less than a minute elapsed between his stepping out the front door and him leaping back inside. He tore the dagger from his coat, thinking balefully of investing in a handgun, and checked every window and door twice before returning to the bedroom.

Johan slept on as Mason paced. The blade was only stowed away as Johan began to scrub his eyes, timed with the first notes of dawn across the sky. He had only a moment to rise before Mason was in his face. If the boy cringed from his true dead stare this time, so be it. It was taking everything not to have the young widower's throat now and drag the morose aftermath along with him as a squealing shield.

He settled for taking Johan's shoulders in his hands and letting the ice of them dig in.

"Johan."

"Mason..?"

"This will sound odd, but I'm being serious." Fresh memories of delivery after delivery over the week came back to him. Movers, boxes, grocery bags, a chain of branded vehicles coming one after the other, day after day. Days in which he had not left the house. Nights in which he had stayed in to dress the rooms. He hadn't seen the exterior in full since yesterday when, grudgingly, he had supervised the mowing of the wild grass. Yesterday. That had been *yesterday*. "Are there flowers growing outside my house?"

Sensible worry twisted into confusion on Johan's face. The uncertainty of one who thinks he must have misheard or simply hasn't woken up yet. No time for that.

Mason shook him once, hard. His hands gripped to the edge of bruising.

"*Answer me.*"

"Yes! Yes, alright, there were flowers, what about it?" Johan pried at Mason's hands with his own. "What the hell is wrong with you?" Mason wasn't in the mindset to spin a viable lie. Even if he were, he wasn't sure how an actor on his best day could improvise a connection between his stalker and the sudden garden that had cropped up overnight in his yard.

Overnight, yes. Right outside his house.

What a busy bee was Mr. Morse.

Mason let Johan go, but his hands didn't quite unlock from their claws. He turned and stalked to the window. Just to be sure it really was as bad as he thought. He had only seen the fruits of the front yard's work, after all. He looked through the glass and swallowed back nausea. There was the proof that his new flowerbeds were virulent as much as verdant.

Wild roses frothed here. Garlic blossoms puffed there. A sapling ash tree grew high like an upended stake waiting for something to be pierced on it. And he hadn't noticed. How had he not noticed? Even if some trick of angles had kept the flora out of sight when he opened the door to Johan yesterday, surely he'd have smelled it all. He had been breathing and talking at the time. So how?

For Johan to have seen them, then they must have been mere seedlings at the time. Low and scentless and unbudded. Which meant they had foamed up in full out of the dirt while the two of them were inside. Under twenty-four hours. That was all it took. By this impossible clock, the ash sapling might be a full tree within a day. Perhaps less than that.

Mason was startled back to himself by the sound of the bedroom door clicking shut. Footsteps descended in the distance. Mason made it to the top of the stairs just as Johan was tying his laces before the front door. His messenger bag was already slung on.

"Johan—,"

"I'll send you whatever I can get out of this." Johan didn't look up at him even as he descended the steps, but brandished Magnus' little pocket journal before tucking it carefully away in the bag. "Thanks for a lovely time." His attempt to shut the door was stopped short by Mason's hand.

"Johan, wait." Johan did not wait. Johan didn't even look up enough to notice the change in the flowers, but cut a steady line to his car. Mason, surprised at his own haste, shadowed him in no more than a robe. "Let me explain," he said, not yet knowing how or what to explain, but hating that the words sounded sickeningly like, *Don't leave me alone.*

Johan only mumbled a hoarse, "Not again." He opened the driver's side door—and stopped. Surprise and worry opened his eyes wide. Finally, he looked up. Accusation crowded into his expression on top of everything else. "Was this you?" Mason circled around to his side and looked where Johan pointed. If his heart still beat, it would have halted fast enough to hurt.

A nest had been made in the driver's seat. Bloodied antique wedding lace was folded into a bed where all manner of little prizes roosted. Familiar engagement rings and faded playing cards. Newsprint obituaries and missing persons reports going back through lifetimes. Photographs, all in that elderly Kodak monochrome. Headstones and tombs and markers of all kinds across numerous countries. The one at the top of the bundle was a shot of an old dual plot.

Here lay the young lord Aubrey and his sister, died a day apart in April of 1819. Red pen was scrawled across the stones:

The dead travel fast. But not forever.

All of this was, naturally, wreathed with a garland of certain flowers. Frowning, Johan plucked one of the garlic blossoms and twisted it in his fingers.

"Do you want to try and explain this? Mason?" he asked. Possibly. Mason was having trouble registering that he was still on Earth, let alone standing next to him. What little blood there was in him had all dropped down to his feet. The morning tilted in his eyes or else his brain tilted in his skull. Either way, the ground was trying to come up and catch him. "Mason!"

Johan caught him before he thought to steady himself against the car's hood. Hunger pangs ran up and down every underfed artery. Slowly, the slate of his stare moved to find Johan's face. Concerned all over again. Poor Mason, poor Mason. Whatever can he do to help?

Mason looked at Johan Teller's throat and watched the Adam's apple dance nervously below his chin.

He wondered who else was watching.

Waiting.

Daring him.

"I need to be somewhere else," he finally murmured as the sun threw its golden light on a new day. From the corner of his eye, he saw an ash leaf drift by on a warm breeze. "Please take me somewhere else."

IX

"We still need to get some actual authorities on this, you know." Johan threw him a look as he shook out his guest bed's sheets. "There has to be something more they can do than take another note." He smoothed the covers with more violence than they needed and huffed, "'Oh no, that sounds awful. Thanks for the update, let us know when he kills one of you and we can get right on it.'"

"That's about the size of it in my experience," Mason shrugged. "If there was anything else they felt like doing, it would have been done already." He frowned at his overnight bag still sitting in the desk chair. He'd set it down gently enough that the blades wouldn't make a sound. "Which does say something about you, I think."

Johan looked up from where he was shaking a pillow into its case.

"How's that?"

"Someone saner would have either left me passed out on the ground or kicked me out at another hotel. At a guess," which was no guess, for he could taste the truth, "you have a habit of playing knight."

"Not really. Damsel now and then. Sometimes a squire. But you *are* being targeted by someone with a fixation and he didn't make a move last night when he likely could have. Maybe it was because he knew somebody else was there. Could be that spoils it for him somehow. Certainly seems shy enough when you aren't by yourself."

"That's a word for it. Anything I should know as far as house rules?"

"Always replace an empty roll, don't invite any strangers, and don't go poking around in the room to the right of mine. It's locked for a reason."

"Which is?"

"It's Arthur's room. Or was." Again, the worrying touch at the wedding band. Again, the hypnotic lurch of his throat. "Now it's where all my work is. So."

"Understood."

Johan stopped in the doorway, chewing on a thought. Then:

"If you're not calling the police yet, you should at least ring your professor friend. If your shadow's going out of his way to leave me little surprises, then there's a chance he stopped by there too."

"Yes. I suppose there is."

Time crawled. Time sprinted. Time melted.

Time turned minutes into what felt like years and weeks into mere blinks. Mason Darvell had seen others endure such in their finicky 'dry spells' as they fussed over just the right meal. This sugared maiden, that strapping youth, someone of particular character or look or taste. Mason was no such gourmand. Some meals were there just to fill one's mouth, others were there to enjoy by increments, and the two rarely overlapped. As one month fattened into two, he tried to rationalize his fasting in a dozen ways. All of them leaned into one of two purposes.

One: He was waiting for the right moment to drain Johan Teller to his last drop. He was clearly working himself into such a ravenous state that, when the time came, he would fasten on him like a starving lamprey and drink the boy hollow. Full exsanguination in a single draught. The relief of quenched thirst would marry with the high of the boy's terror and strike Mason like an intoxicating shot directly to the brain.

· Two: He feared the repercussions of Quinn Morse. No longer a cat playing with a mouse, but a heavy boot coming down on a cockroach. Each night brought more certainty that the bastard was waiting for him to make just the right wrong move. To transgress and set off some prearranged tripwire of his or his master's that would permit the hunt to resume in earnest. Surely that pointed to a divine power. The trick with the sickening flora had to point that way too. Didn't it?

The uncertainty gnawed as deeply as the hunger at times. He ignored it best when he was playing increasingly frustrated detective.

"1893, London. 1893, London. 1893, London." A mantra whispered when he knew Johan to be out of earshot or, horribly, out of the house. Mason had brought his own tablet from home and only used it for research when he felt reasonably sure his host wouldn't amble into the room. Whenever he wasn't with Mason or out and about, Johan was locked in his office with his job and the project of Magnus' journal. Mason wasn't even certain anymore if a translation mattered. There was no guarantee that it contained any allusion to Mr. Morse's reality. For all he knew, it could just be an idle diary recording the ugly unmaking of Magnus' victims. Yet Johan never returned green-faced from his work.

"About a third through," he'd announce. Then half. Three-quarters.

"Anything interesting?"

"A bit. Reads like the owner was either trying his hand at a patchy horror novel or maybe downed a few too many classic cokes back in the day."

Ha ha.

Ha.

Back to the tablet. 1893, London. Mason stopped bothering with 'murder' as a connecting topic after a fruitless spree spent being redirected to stale Jack the Ripper theory pieces. Research of strange occurrences were more fruitful, though it turned up nothing particularly grisly. Nor did the events all land neatly in London's heart. Instead, intuition seemed to sketch a rough daisy chain of happenings starting out on the quiet shore of Whitby.

Here was the ghost ship Demeter and its dead captain tied to the wheel. A freakish storm had pushed the vessel to shore that summer before a massive hound leapt from it and disappeared.

There was a lull between this event and the far end of September when the 'Hampstead Horror,' made her appearance, likewise dubbed 'the Bloofer Lady.' A pretty maiden who spent her nights enticing children away to play before abandoning them dazed and half-alive to be found by whoever might scoop them up. Her career had ended almost as abruptly as it began. Put down by some party who had known her for what she was and knew where to find her in her sleep.

Here were obituaries turning up an abundance of young women in the area to choose from, plenty of whom had consumption as their cause of death. While there were no photos to point the way, there was the expected pomp of peerage to boost some above the rabble. After much sifting, his more than natural insight drew him toward Miss Lucille Westenra and her mother, both having died a heartbeat apart. The matron to shock, the daughter to some ill-defined malady of the blood. As an aside, their deaths were preceded by the freak incident of a wolf smashing through a window of their stately abode.

Trying to scrounge through the finer details beyond the sensationalism of the story was a moot effort. There was no finding who had overseen the funeral, nor the names of the doctors tied with her diagnosis. But there was at least one prominent mourner's name tied to the date of her being slotted into the family crypt.

A newly minted Lord Arthur Godalming, her fiancé while she lived. There was little enough to find of him elsewhere. There were few other brushes with death beyond those in aristocratic circles. This included a close friend by the name of Dr. John Seward who'd passed away as an old man in Purfleet. And in younger days, buried on American soil...

Mason almost cracked the tablet in half. He read the section again. Three times. Four. It didn't change.

Quincey Morris. Son of a sizeable cattle ranch empire in Texas, he'd dropped the reins and the hereditary business to travel, adventure, and, in November of 1893, die under mysterious circumstances in Europe. Transylvania, to be specific. Tragically slain by some common criminal while he and some friends, including Lord Godalming, were out on a tour of the country. He had bled out.

But just as hope of a lead began to simmer, it was snuffed by a wall where further information should have been. Photographs, personal activities, friends of intriguing background—none could be dredged up. Mason tried to tell himself it was still progress. An American, a *Texan* no less, might be lazy enough to sand down his living name into a pseudonym while playing vengeful spirit, replete with the old black hat and duster. But what did some errant cowboy know about the occult? What deal could he have made before or after dying in the Carpathian snow that could make him a worthy recipient of the supernatural?

"Could be necromancy," he mouthed to himself.

Quietly, quietly. Johan was making dinner. He'd not questioned Mason's insistence that he prepare his own nonexistent meals or that he eat alone. Always while Johan was out or shut in the office, naturally. The boy seemed resigned to Mason Darvell's assorted oddities of character and to never receiving any answer that wasn't a lie or some fresh round of madness. Supposing an answer could be wrung out of Mason at all these days. As the fasting wore on, his persona wore down with it. So it had always gone when he deprived himself even a week too long.

A threshold he'd passed some weeks ago.

Now he was positively arid on the inside. A mummy would be more hydrated than the straining mess under his own skin. He made only the barest effort at character when Johan interacted with him. The odd card game could let him pass his deadening off as concentration while worry about Mr. Morse could disguise it with apparent glumness. But all other hours were devoted to a spiral between the inactivity of a true corpse or the shudder and twitch of a deprived addict.

Then go on, hissed the thirst. *Go out to hunt. Go to the boy. Get on with it. Get on with* something, *damn you.*

He didn't. Sometimes he would get close. He would dress, he would go out the door as Johan slept or worked, he would search the air for a whiff of soul and sustenance, he would make it to a promising street or viable window with some supple young thing waiting for his steel.

And then *he* would be there.

On a wall. Atop a roof. In the alley. At his shoulder. The face still a shadow with burning corpse eyes, white hair hanging like a funeral shroud beneath the broad brim. It was almost down to a science how instantaneous the apparition's presence became whenever Mason dared to slink close enough to his spigot of choice. Not that he ever managed a cut. Not so much as a word was exchanged before that awful arctic stare was on him again.

Back home he would rush. Trying with ever weaker arguments to convince himself he was not followed or going insane or withering himself down to a husk of mobile death. The one time he'd tried to wring a response out of Mr. Morse had been half a week ago, back when he still had energy to waste on speech not directed at Johan.

"Quincey Morris," he'd rasped. "That's your true name, isn't it?" Said as if the notion carried any weight. As though he were some malevolent fairy who could be banished by guessing his real title. Quinn Morse had said nothing to him. Instead, he unslung a Winchester. "*Talk* to me, at least. Tell me what you want. Is this for you or another?" Quinn Morse loaded the chamber. Blessed silver gleamed. "Say something!" The Winchester aimed. Mason ran.

Mr. Morse hadn't even bothered to waste the shot. Not with a bullet.

Mason found the wound waiting for him when he made it back to Johan's front door. He discovered a photograph pinned under a rock on the doormat. A simple shot of an overgrown grave. The weathered stone had lost something of the surname, but the top displayed the name *Ianthe*. Red pen was scrawled below it:

Again, baffled.

Mason shredded the image into flakes. Then trudged in to sit through a movie with Johan.

His host had an admittedly dusty taste, preferring films that began life as plays. Shakespeare and Marlowe reproductions would often be put on as background noise. He was less than enthused to find that the most recent choice was Richard Burton languishing his way through 1967's *Doctor Faustus*.

"You can turn it off if you like," Johan had hummed as he tapped away at the keyboard in his lap. "It's practically hate-watching at this point."

"Why's that?" Mason had asked, if only to make a responsive noise. He watched a cloud move over Johan's face while a thunderhead boomed in his mind. It tasted of acerbic old rage that had been planted long ago and left to fester.

"I've never liked the premise, even as a moral story. Faustus, this supposed genius, learns the Devil is real enough to sell his soul to. Rather than doing the sane thing and *not* arbitrarily chucking himself at the Inferno, he immediately barters his eternity away for a few decades of magic tricks. Then, surprise, he dies and goes to Hell, as per the contract. I know it's a stupid thing to nitpick. 'Shocking! Local sinner and fool sells himself to the Devil, gets hell-bound!' It's obvious, it's a classic moralistic storytelling framework, whatever."

He closed his laptop with a somehow venomous *clack*. The thunderhead was now working itself into a full storm. Mason almost felt the electric prickle of it.

"The frustrating thing is that it's *always* pitched as a tragedy. It isn't." He gestured at the screen where Burton was asking if Elizabeth Taylor's face was the one that launched a thousand ships. "His only hamartia is that, oh, whoops, he tripped and signed his name in blood and, oh no, he went and ignored the reality of Hell until the *last second* when he has to uphold his end of the deal he made while being *explicitly told what the terms were*. No fine print! No loopholes! No knife to his throat or infernal peril muscling him into it! Just paper and print from Satan himself stating everything in black and white while God's own angels and Mephistopheles himself begged him not to do it. And we're supposed to grieve for him?"

Johan got to his feet with the remote in hand, holding the length of plastic as if he wished it were a pistol. Mason's eyes almost rolled back as wave upon wave of loathing and regret rolled over him. Even if it didn't sate hunger, it struck like morphine.

"If Marlowe wanted tragedy," Johan all but spat, "he should have swapped Faustus for the kind of victim that gods and devils would actually bother with."

"What victim is that?" Mason asked placidly enough. His hands were shaking.

The storm gave way to an apocalypse roiling across the terrain of Johan Teller's mind. A huge and delectable misstep had been made somewhere in his history and there had been no recovery. Mason inhaled it with the vigor of a man bent over lines of white powder as Johan glowered at the screen.

"The kind who wouldn't have been set for Hell otherwise. Faustus could have damned himself easily enough with or without supernatural interference. But someone desperate, someone willing to haggle themselves away to save—," his throat leapt and jerked, and Mason saw his stare had gone bloodshot, "—to do some impossible good deed that every other circumstance in the world is stacked against? That's the kind of target who gets preyed on every day." Then, under his breath, "With or without a fucking contract."

Johan switched off the TV rather than kicking a hole through it. He managed to make this look like a Herculean accomplishment. Mason listened to him retreat to the office, unlock the door, and shut it curtly after him. Half a minute after the door's internal bolt slid home, Mason was pressed up against the heavy wood, siphoning the vapor trail of raw hurt and hate still thrumming in the air. A gossamer thread of drool grew from his bottom lip. Soon, soon, soon he would...

He'd...

A drop of saliva fell and broke on the floorboards.

What are you doing?

It was a question that echoed on into the night.

The day after. The night after that. At the end of the next day, there was still no answer. Not until he paused in flipping the wall calendar to the next month—June to July—and realized he was holding paper proof that he had spent two months in that house without drinking. Not unless one counted the night before, when he had poked a thumbnail through the plastic wrapping on a slab of beef in the fridge and sucked the bovine juices out like a tick.

Mason took himself to the mirror in the guest room and tried to find himself in the glass. He wasn't there. Some imposter filled the frame instead. A figure who might have been handsome, if pallid, just over ten weeks ago. Now he was an overripe specimen for an anatomy class. A greyed and sunken shape that finally matched his eyes. What's the COD, class? Anyone, anyone?

Dehydration. Starvation. Lunacy.

Lunacy, yes. The moon could make a body sick to death in brain and blood and bone, it makes some men mad and some men monsters and now after all these centuries it was grinding his sanity down to a fine pulp, it had dug up a dead thing with its hair all

shock and lunar light and sent it to carve his world apart with
a crescent moon in one hand and a shooting star in the other,
revolving around and around and around him until he was so bereft
of borrowed blood he would have to break himself open and be his
own ouroboros nursing from the marrow until the woeful widower
walked in and asked if there was anything he could do, would he
like a straw for that, would he—

Mason tipped his head back before smashing it hard against
the glass. Cracks flowered in all directions. Shards flew loose. In the
least shattered portion of the glass, he could see he'd managed to
cut himself. Yet no blood ran. Not a single drop. Something else
was flowing in there now. Something vital.

Recognition.

In the glass there was more than his haggard face. What he
saw there was the gawping, lingering, enamored stares of an endless
chain of lovers and would-be slayers who had made the lethal
mistake of looking upon parasitic beauty. Stalled from running,
halted in the act of bringing down stake or steel. Stayed and stared.
Stayed and dwindled. Stayed and maddened.

Stayed and died.

Two months.

Two months.

How long had Kate lasted before the end?

"*He's here and he's real,*" Mason echoed to the broken glass.
"*Quinn Morse was a cover.*"

X

Despite the magnitude of the moment, it really was only a moment. Between the sound of the smashing glass and the hasty padding of steps from the office there was only a space of six seconds. Yet it was enough to prepare. He was ready when Johan knocked and called through the door.

"Mason, are you alright in there? I heard something break."

"I'm fine," he called back. "Had a little accident with the mirror." He tied his robe and opened the door on Johan's appropriately worried face. His line of sight found the mirror first. Then he took in the new bloodless gash on Mason's brow and his mien changed to aghast perfection.

"God, did you fall?" His hand reached up. "There's still a piece here." His hand was caught. "Mason?" He pulled. Mason's grip grew tight enough to make the wrist creak. "Mason." A smaller tone this time. The kind reserved for talking down a dog with its hackles up. "I need you to let me go now. Then I think we need to get you to a doctor. You need stitches and," he winced again, less from pain than from the whole view of the man before him, "I don't know, some kind of examination. You're starting to look awful."

"Not awful. Dead. You can say it. I look dead." Mason's lips peeled back in a mirthless curl. "About time, isn't it? You have been *so* patient. So meticulous. How long did it take for Kate? She must have looked awful even before you let him have her."

Johan stopped trying to pry Mason's hand off him and gawked. His face said fear. His smell said only bewildered surprise.

"What?"

"No need to play innocent at this point. Not when you've taken so much already. You'll leave barely a crumb for Mr. Morris at the rate you're glutting yourself on me, you leech."

More confusion sweated from Johan even as the first lines of it showed on his face. It had to be a false impression. Some tailored thing. Kate would have known the name for it. A glamour of the mind or suchlike. It didn't matter. It was a lie. Every sweet and supple dose of gloom from him was so much poisoned honey.

"Morris? Do you mean Morse?" Speaking softer, lower. Easy boy, down boy, no biting. Ha. *Ha.* "Mason, I'm really not following you here."

"You are. You have been. You followed me to Belchamp. Or does *he* lead the way? Would that make him a bloodhound, do you think?" He crushed until the wrist screamed and Johan made a sharp noise between his teeth. Mason bared his own teeth back. The boy's eyes went wide at the sight of the spires growing from their pale gums. "*What is he? Is he yours or are you his? Answer me, you walking tumor.*"

Unhappy wonder had turned to a blank slate now. The sort of hollowness that Mason sometimes scented in those most annoying victims who, upon seeing the reality of him in full, simply refused to believe what they saw. They were dreaming, is all. How odd. They were certain they'd been awake a moment ago. It always dampened the taste of them. Johan Teller would not rob him of that too.

"*Start talking.*" His other hand left the terrycloth pocket. Also gripping its catch tight. "*It's only a matter of time before I hit the heart.*"

Johan opened his mouth to form another inane question. It opened wider to release the first scream.

There was air and energy enough for only a handful more. None of them were answers. All he offered were broken vowels occasionally interspersed with Mason's name. In the brief time Mason had for retrospect, he would muse that hunger and rage had turned him sloppy. Normally an artist with his steel, the dagger attacked Johan like a drunken butcher. One of the earliest cuts had split the young man's neck with so deep a slice that he could see a flash of vertebrae in the slit. But perhaps he'd imagined that glimpse. His mind became a frenzied haze after that wound released the fountain of the carotid artery.

Oh, O! The boy was candy! Ambrosia! There was no treat dangled before Tantalus that could match that scarlet flow. Mason lost track of the minutes spent nursing every ounce that welled to the split skin, mourning all those that were lost to the young man's shirtfront and floor. He pondered going on all fours and lapping the mess up on hands and knees. And then stopped.

He looked down into Johan Teller's dark eyes. They stared back.

"Come on, vampyre. I didn't hit the heart. Get up."

Johan Teller was still.

"Do you need the moon as well? Is that it? Or are you waiting for him to smash in the window and skin me for ending the game too soon? I feel worlds better. I could be across the Channel before the sun's up. Would he linger a while if he found you here? Would he tend you or carve you?"

Johan Teller didn't say. Or blink. Or breathe.

"I could almost sympathize if it was a 'you or us' arrangement, you know. I'd have done the same if I had your option. I've never met one of our ilk who could feed off the others. A rather tedious form of playing incubus, but effective. Very effective. For a time." He made a low rumbling sound that passed for a chuckle.

Johan Teller remained silent. It occurred to Mason that his mind had been just as hushed when the steel began to open him up. No true emotion beyond little flares of exclamation or hope. A flicker-flash of reaching for something not in the room, something beyond the pain and its giver. Perhaps a prayer.

Please...please...please...

Now even that had gone quiet. Blank as a void. And just as dead.

Mason sat back on his haunches, his gaze drifting between the cooling face and the red arch of the dagger abandoned on the floor. He scooped the weapon up to hold it before the bright brown eyes. Its point brushed the fringe of lashes before tucking away a loose strand of hair.

"I'll do it. I'm not joking."

Johan Teller declined to say whether he believed him or not. Not even when the dagger slid first one, then two, then three inches deep between his ribs. Mason slid the entire blade into the slack heart until hilt met chest. There was no spontaneous rot. No champing of sudden new fangs. No elemental dust. Nothing. Just a corpse with a knife in it. Mason felt cold disappointment pour through him.

The boy was now what he'd always been: only human.

Worse, he'd died as he lived, a sacrifice to wasted patience and idiot assumptions.

Damn him.

"No time for this," Mason hissed. It would be just like his dear flaxen friend to show up now that he was red-handed. Along with red-lipped, chinned, faced. "Focus." He scrambled up and over Johan's body, forcing himself not to lick his mouth and palms clean like a child. He'd need to wash, stuff everything in the overnight bag, and make his way to another refuge. A hotel or the brownstone over in Piccadilly? He'd flip a coin in Johan's car.

This thought sparked another and he doubled back to Johan's body to grope in the pockets. He found the keys on his first grab, clutching the ring gingerly. But then his eye caught on something else. The oldest key in the small bunch, sandwiched between car fob and housekey. A brassy little thing meant for a specific lock. It occurred to Mason that, even with this being such a solid old Victorian box of a house, the office door was the only one to have its original doorknob in place. He'd written it off as some sentimental historian's whim, wanting to preserve something of the 19th century while so many advanced odds and ends were laced through the rest of the structure.

On the heels of this, it also occurred to him that the office door was between him and Magnus' notebook. Another thing he had written off while time passed and his senses dissolved into a bog of dread and dalliance. Johan really had been taking his sweet time poking through the pages, hadn't he? Supposedly flicking through leaf after leaf between work and food and sleep and playing host. It was past time to collect whatever was done and push the rest off on a hastier hobbyist.

Mason rushed on light feet to the office, turned the key, and got as far as swinging the door open before a spasm of displeasure slammed through him from the feet up. The atrophied ball of his stomach lurched. His skin shuddered on his flesh so violently it nearly crawled off. He twisted away and looked down.

The hardwood floor had been marred just inside the doorframe. A line of pale crumbs and a recognizable medley of potpourri had been sprinkled before the door. It was laid out beside a row of symbols carved into the wood. Crosses and stars, sigils and wards, Abrahamic and far older. Mason could feel the barbs of the latter scratched just inside the frame along the walls and ceiling. Across the room he saw the same etching along the windowsill, likewise dusted down with the same petals and Eucharist powder.

There, waiting in the warm spotlight of a desk lamp, was Count Magnus' little journal. It rested like a feeble paperweight atop Johan's larger personal volume. A scattered heap of pages had been half-tumbled from the desk, along with a broad discarded envelope. Knocked askew in the jolt of hearing the breaking mirror. Pity.

Mason Darvell's mind battled between the barrenness of shock and the entropy of trying to divulge all the implied potentialities now in front of him.

One, they *were* together. Johan and Quinn.

Two, they *weren't* together. Morse had laid all this out while Mason was busy with the slaughter down the hall. The transgression giving him some magic impetus to act in earnest rather than playing with his food.

Three, Johan Teller was his own superstitious animal and had done the work himself.

The last theory was dismissed even as it came to him. Human hands had flung these and worse at him as would-be protection. At best he had suffered the equivalent of an allergic reaction. But the graffiti at the door made him nauseous to the point of utter revulsion. It was potent, pungent, powerful. A hard arcane cudgel against the senses. *Turn back*, it said. *Keep out.*

Morse. It had to be Morse.

Mason retreated two long steps, then threw himself over the threshold with a strangled howl. It sickened. It ached. It needled the beginnings of a monstrous migraine behind his eyes. But now, at last, he was somewhere Quinn Morse clearly did not want him to be. He stumbled more than walked to the desk and its spill of papers. His hand went for the fallen envelope first, planning to stuff the wad of sheets inside to be made sense of elsewhere.

The envelope crinkled fragilely under his touch. Mason saw now that its paper was startlingly old. As old as the typewritten sheets spread in a white-black sea around it. He scooped a sheaf of them up gingerly, frowning at the texture and the spotty marks of a typewriter that had chewed the pages out unknown decades ago. Perhaps more than a century. His eyes hopped wildly as he flipped through at random. He couldn't help landing on certain sections that had been defaced with red ink. Underlined passages, circled paragraphs, question marks, and the decoration of increasingly desperate inquiry all clogged the margins.

> What manner of man is this, or what manner of creature is it in the semblance of man? I feel the dread of this horrible place overpowering me; I am in fear—in awful fear—and there is no escape for me

> **Desperation striking home. Full acknowledgment of inhumanity. He could smell it, I'm sure. So could It. Spied an opportunity?**

Another page.

> This was the being I was helping to transfer to London, where, perhaps for centuries to come, he might, amongst its teeming millions, satiate his lust for blood, and create a new and ever-widening circle of semi-demons to batten on the helpless. The very thought

drove me mad. A terrible desire came upon me to rid the world of such a monster.

The basilisk trick and the men cut the effort short. Blood loss too great. But that first shovel strike stayed a raw scar for all the months to come. Only a spade. Nothing sacred. Not even a blow to the heart or throat. Yet it lasted on a Thing that had survived the battles and mortal interventions of centuries. How? Did this start so early? Culpability opening the door; guilt and potential. I don't know. I don't know.

Another, another, another, another, all scarred with arterial ink.

Harker was still and quiet; but over his face, as the awful narrative went on, came a grey look which deepened and deepened in the morning light, till when the first red streak of the coming dawn shot up, the flesh stood out starkly against the whitening hair.

Changing for the occasion. Even without putting it into words, It knew. It knew what was in my heart. What I was willing to do, to give. It knew.

To one thing I have made up my mind: if we find out that Mina must be a vampire in the end, then she shall not go into that unknown and terrible land alone.

It knew.

"I care for nothing now," he answered hotly, "except to wipe out this brute from the face of creation. I would sell my soul to do it!"

IT KNEW. Against God, against Hell, against all. Idiot, imbecile! You knew too! In the maelstrom of all these infernal realities, you say this aloud? Idiot!

Harker evidently meant to try the matter, for he had ready his great Kukri knife, and made a fierce and sudden cut at him.

'Sic him, boy.'

Godalming and Morris had rushed out into the yard, and Harker had lowered himself from the window to follow the Count.

'Going out in his lizard fashion.' How much of this is for the cosmic irony versus the duty of it?

"If beyond it I could send his soul forever and ever to burning hell I would do it!"

'Why stop at him?'

In an instant he had jumped upon the cart, and, with a strength which seemed incredible, raised the great box, and flung it over the wheel to the ground.

How many men had to lift it on? Box, soil, man and all. Why did I never think on it?

As I looked, the eyes saw the sinking sun, and the look of hate in them turned to triumph.

But, on the instant, came the sweep and flash of Jonathan's great knife. I shrieked as I saw it shear through the throat; whilst at the same moment Mr. Morris's bowie knife plunged into the heart.

It was like a miracle; but before our very eyes, and almost in the drawing of a breath, the whole body crumbled into dust and passed from our sight.

Payment or the first assignment?

His mother holds, I know, the secret belief that some of our brave friend's spirit has passed into him. His bundle of names links all our little band of men together; but we call him Quincey.

My boy, I know you were there waiting for her. All your namesakes are with you. How do you find Morris? Did he greet you with your godfather? Uncles Art and Jack will have such stories to share between the lot of them. Have you made friends with Aunt Lucy? She would have given her name to you had you been born our daughter. I pray there is a Heaven where you all wait. I pray there is a less callous God presiding than the one who burned your mother's brow for another's sin, the God who let the brute reign unchecked and bloodstained for half a millennium until your fodder of a father threw himself to Powers more stringent than any Lord or Devil to sever his career.

Already he knows her sweetness and loving care; later on he will understand how some men so loved her, that they did dare much for her sake."

Dared. Gave. Giving.

And there, packed in a final sheet:

I will never take it back, never regret what I vowed or what was taken to ensure all. He took too much for forgiveness to ever bud. Perhaps that branded me most. Karma or Its excuse? It doesn't matter. I have been left here to my work either way.

How many more are left? Will the duty ever run dry? The dead always outnumber the living and every day their number increases. What does that mean for the undead? I shudder each time I try to picture the list.

Death does not shudder. It hates. It frowns over Its cheated ledger each time a rite or a bite robs the queue, each time the dead make prey of the living in perversion of Its laws. Now It suffers the idleness of the Divine and the caprices of the Diabolic no more. It has found Itself new help at a bargain. It will not let him quit.

Hold our boy for me, my darling. Tell him I will put his old gifts from Uncle Morris to good use. Yes, even his most beloved accessory. I cannot bear to see it resting on his pillow anymore. I cannot tell whether I look foolish in it and the ensemble or not. Camera and mirror decline to show me in whole once I'm in my working condition. I suppose that doesn't matter either. The only witnesses have little enough time to share their opinions.

I try where I can for quickness. So few make the choice themselves and fewer still find their delight in making it a cruel sport. But those who do?

No. I will not linger on it. You know. Surely you know, wherever you are now. I will not ask forgiveness from you for the measures I take to feed them their own cruel venom. Would I even see you again should the day come that I finish here? Would I have earned that with my servitude or would it be barred for some crime of my own bile imposed on those horrors who persist solely to inflict themselves on innocents? Neither would surprise me.

Somewhere I have gone awry. That or I have been blithely swatted and stolen off the route we once walked together. Simply because I was there and ripe for use. For the greater good, of course.

Mina.

Mina.

Even now I cannot repent you. My gods were older than Scripture even if I didn't know it. But at least Lenore was allowed to die despite her loving sin. Perhaps someday I will be permitted. I have tolls to spare for my quarry and they are my toll in turn. So I hope.

Mason looked between this and the worn little pocket journal with eyes that had begun aching in earnest. Johan Teller's journal sat under it. It seemed to be watching him. He felt Pandora's soul sink into his bones and walk him to the volume. His fingers trembled as he flipped back through page after page of scratched notes. Some English, some shorthand, some scrapbooking.

Between a brilliant photograph of a scenic botanical garden and pasted ticket stubs for an old jewel box theater, he saw a monochrome shot of Kate Northcott's remains in their collapsed spill within her sundress. A parting comment beneath a few rows of shorthand:

Two months and a quarter before it hit. Should have dusted off a 'John' or a 'Jack,' if only to see if she remembered poor Cowles. Probably not.

Another page showed Count Magnus' putrid slurry of flesh and crumbled bone inside his copper box, likewise in an elderly Kodak's shot. It was tucked in beside glossier photos of St. Andrew's.

I can still hear my fellow hireling's laugh. An uncanny artist if nothing else.

Each turn of the page insisted upon another turn back, showing the tourist march in reverse. Solo shots and wide landscapes of villages overtaken by blessed flora.

They smile when it's a group. Every time. Plagues unending, ended.

So it went, page by page, up to the very beginning.

Kodak shot.

Two graves, beautifully kept.

Arthur John Abraham 'Quincey' Harker
Cherished Son
Lived and Loved with Spirit
November 1896—May 1919

Wilhelmina 'Mina' Harker
Beloved Wife, Mother, Friend
Much was Dared for Her, She Dared Far More
August 1873—November 1923

Mason cradled the book with numb hands. He was starting to wobble. The room afflicted like toxic fumes. Out. Had to get out. Think later, but do it *out*, do it *away*...

He took the journal in both hands and tore it in half. He did the same for its palm-sized ancestor. The typed sheets and all their annotations were shredded into snow. He snapped the slab of the laptop in two. When he upended the hefty scholar's desk, he was as unsurprised as he was livid to see what its drawers spilled. A drawstring bag tumbled loose, spilling ancient gold coins. Roman and British, Austrian and Hungarian, Greek and Turkish. Mason kicked them in a twinkling spray. His heel crunched a framed photograph of a sitting mother and child where both sat distracted by a picture book. Frozen in sepia, they were torn by his sole and the glass.

His eye fell on the walls themselves and saw he'd missed more prizes. Each was bookended by dried hangings of rose, garlic, and ash.

Framed: A woman smiles tiredly out of her sea of downy covers and pillows. Illness has siphoned more life from her than time could, turning mid-life creases into the premonitions of decay. Her eyes still glitter as she looks up at a familiar young man who clasps her thin hand in both of his. His smile is paltry compared to hers, but his eyes are brighter jewels for their pain. Their wedding bands match. Only the two men in the background, each stamped in their own woe, bother to wear cloth masks while the young man bows close, hoping to inhale some of her tainted breath. His hair is streaked with white.

Framed: Family portrait. Mother is merry. Her adolescent boy is laughing, tipping the brim of a broad black hat on his head. The young man stands beside him, slightly taller, looking more like a brother than a father. His hair is dark.

Framed: A landscape of snow-capped mountains. The ruins of a castle roost in the rock. In the foreground, a row of people stand facing the camera the way huntsmen might pose beside a slain beast. Here is an old man of bushy brows and stout strongman build, but buttoned into the tidy tailoring of a professor under his coat. Beside him is a youngish fellow of hawkish eyes and sharp angles, struggling to look sociable for the camera, and his comrade, a misplaced aristocrat with wild Cupid curls swept out of the way of a Leyendecker face. A young woman—destined to be mother, to be morgue-bound before her time—smiles arm and arm with her young man at the far end of the line. A fellow of chipper smile, haunted eyes, and white hair with creeping threads of dark brown. In his other arm he balances an infant just stretching into toddlerhood, a little hand grasping at the wild rose in his father's lapel.

Framed: Most of these odd characters, all of them bunched into a single room as they huddle in a strange conference. The room is scraped straight from some cluttered Victorian parlor. The one addition is a man with his black hat tipped back so that it clings by the cord about his neck. His complexion marks him as one of America's southern sons, Texan, Mexican, or the fruit of both, while his whole manner is of one born for slaying dragons. A revolver sits prominently on his hip, the holster emblazoned with a stylized M. Only the as-yet-unborn child and the scene's photographer are missing from the shot, the latter forced by the Kodak's design to lurk behind the lens.

Red ink was scratched along the bottom.

September, 1893. *The beginning of his end.*

Even so close to the glass, Mason almost didn't notice the reflection hovering behind his own. In fairness, there was nearly no reflection to work with. His only warning was the shine of its eyes.

Not that the warning was much help when a sharp length of steel was abruptly slotted through the back of Mason's neck until it filled his throat like a second tongue. He gagged and turned in time to see the last of Johan Teller fading away.

The pallor of a corpse greyed out the warmth of the umber face while the dark curtain of hair bleached to shock white. The eyes had burned away every hint of the human iris. Unreadable hating blankness dwelled behind that stare. An endless pit that was Death's own maw.

"Jo—," was as far as Mason got before he felt the rot starting to creep out from the knife. "Jo—Jon—,"

The thing that was not Johan Teller any more than it was Quinn Morse had no words to spare for him. Only another addition to share with Mason's anatomy.

Mason keened around the spreading black mush in his throat as the shaft of an ash spear punched through his torso and into the wall. He scrabbled at this and the handle of the knife as his host strolled over to the door, moving it just enough to show the hook hanging on its back. A weathered black hat and accompanying coat hung there. Cold hands rooted for something in one of the duster's hidden folds.

With his back turned, Mason saw that there was a scabbard on one hip. A holster hung on the other side with its flap unbuttoned above the grip.

"I can't tell anymore why I take my time with you," a tired voice intoned. "Seward would've had something to say about it, I'm sure. 'It's to repay the torment of the victims. All the time spent dragging out regard and agony to a miserable end.'" A handful of monochrome photos was found and flung aside. More headstones foraged throughout England and Europe. He continued to rummage. "'It's bitterness that you would choose this. It's taking joy where you can.' Perhaps that's part of it." Mason sank his fangs into his lip so hard it tore, then began pulling himself forward. All the while trying not to think of the decomposed spill that was already growing where his bowels used to be. "You have so much in common with my first, you know. He lingered on me too. He did much worse than linger. But I never did get to give him all he gave me." Still searching. Back still turned. "It seems a feasible enough excuse."

New blood stained the wood as Mason dragged. His left hand went again to the knife's handle, groping and pulling. The blade was straighter than any of his daggers. Smoother. He could almost...

"It turns out you're *all* so like him. Which stands to reason. It takes a certain type to strike the deals you have and do what you do for sport."

Almost. If he could just ignore the crumbling. The stench. The cold. *Almost.*

"I like to believe that's the reason I take these detours most days. Belated justice and all. But the truth is, with your lot in the old guard, all you undead and immortal bargainers, I think I give you so much time and madness and a length of rope to tie because I hope one of you might finally do the impossible. I hope that some night, one of you could actually do better than—,"

Now.

In a single lurch he was off the length of ash, the knife was torn from the decay at his nape, and his right hand was leading the way in a desperate blur. The revolver came into his palm with a sweep. In the same instant, he fired a bullet through the skull under the shag of white hair. A burst of blood, bone, and brain painted the hanging coat. One heartbeat came and went.

Mason watched him turn around. A tunnel had opened up in the center of his forehead. Red rivers trailed down his face. It did little to improve the irritation stamped there.

"—disappoint me."

To punctuate this, the revolver was confiscated. Likewise the hand holding it.

Mason wrenched away from him with a reedy shrill that would have been a scream but for the sick-softness of the decomposition. The hand that had been holding the knife now went to clutching the dripping stump of the opposite wrist. When the blade hit the floor, the connoisseur in him noticed that it was a sizeable Bowie. One that sported just as clean an edge as the kukri.

He didn't notice the latter's second swipe until it had gone through him. The cut opened a new rotting seam through his middle and dropped him to the floor. When he looked up, he was met by the sight of the bullet's exit wound knitting itself shut on the bloody brow. The hole was gone entirely by the time the black hat came on, its impenetrable shadow erasing any evidence of a face holding up the eyes' twin glow. He heard the scrape of metal against metal.

The hand unburdened by the kukri rubbed ancient coins together.

Gold.

"I'd believe he was the son of a dragon for that hoard, if nothing else. The money of dead men stolen by a dead monster. The one time I tried to spend it as currency I doubt the poor man at the station even collected it. I was given a train ticket just to be sent away. Quite understandable." The gold coins were lifted until they caught the lamplight. "It's meant for the dead. It will only ever bring bad luck to the living who spend it." The kukri leveled at him like a pointing finger. "You would know. It's no coincidence all your losses at the tables went sour for the winners. So *petty* on top of everything else, Ruthven. I'd think you would share the same room with the Count in Hell. But sin doesn't lead all to the same Pit, does it?" He flicked the coins into the pooling blood. "All our debts are different. All owed to so many Powers that be. All with their own allowances."

The kukri raised.

"All but one."

The night went on. The moon watched. Kodaks of two generations took their commemorative shots. Old messes and new were tidied. Johan Teller was put away. Art Golding was considered. Bram Singer. Jack Sewing. Lucien West. Wilhelm Murray. He settled on none of them just yet. He never did until there was an undead ear to give it to. Tonight he went to bed as himself.

He slept without dreaming, as he always did upon reaching the end of another assignment alive.

Despair still had its own calms.

At least God's mercy is better than that of these monsters, and the precipice is steep and high. At its foot a man may sleep—as a man. Good-bye, all! Mina!
—Jonathan Harker, *Dracula*

...The Coffin Closes

Oh, my good friend Jonathan Harker. I love to see him in peril almost as much as I love to see him carve up the most infamous vampires in all of literature. A precedent set by Stoker himself.

It's a fact that's often disregarded or outright obliterated from many a modern media take which decides it looks cooler to have Van Helsing or the latest Lady Love Interest taking down the Count. But as iconic as hammer and stake are, Dracula was done in by cold hard steel. From kukri and Bowie respectively, much obliged to Mr. Harker and the late Quincey Morris. But enough about the old Drac in the Box. He's been old news for ages. There are wilier and wickeder bloodsuckers to worry about. Though, as the preceding tale displayed, not quite as many as before.

One of many ideas batted around in the book clubs of *Dracula Daily* and *Re: Dracula* was how Jonathan Harker transforms over the course of the novel's later acts. Not just in terms of character development, but in physicality. At the start of the story, Dracula is a white-haired old horror manipulating, imprisoning, and preying on Jonathan, the hale dark-haired youth who's hunted and haunted in the castle walls. But by the end of the narrative, it's the white-haired, burning-eyed, wall-crawling, coffin-chucking, blade-swinging Jonathan who falls on Dracula like an eerie living guillotine and lops his head off.

A lot of juicy what-ifs and maybes are explored in *The Vampyres*, at least as far as some of my own theories go. Stoker left all kinds of ingredients laying around the cryptic kitchen to work with. Having poor Jonathan not only pay dearly for an accidental Faustian slip of the tongue in a story where heavenly and hellish Powers are proven to be *very* real, but *also* taking the rightful Tragic Monster Hunter crown as his own felt like the best kind of bittersweet result. Plus, Ruthven's been running around for centuries with barely a blip on the bloodsucker scene. The guy deserved to be dusted off, if only to get dust-to-dusted.

Of course, this is all the fruit of a single idea that's been gnawing at me with needling little bat teeth.

This whole novella was originally intended to be a single short story in a heap of other supernatural tales I've been cobbling together from the parts I robbed from assorted classic horror graves. But as brevity and I are rarely on speaking terms, those shorts run the risk of bloating out of control too. Whether I have to start breaking things up into their own standalones or if I squash everything together into a heftier volume remains to be seen. For now, I'm happy to test the waters of peddling paranormal pages with this sample.

I hope you liked the read and that you'll enjoy any other undead offerings I drag up to your door. If you invite them in, that's on you.

Acknowledgments

I'd like to give a more elaborate thanks to Matt Kirkland for *Dracula Daily* and all it's resulted in. Not just for punting me into my current obsessions, but for beautifully preceding the minor *Dracula* Renaissance taking place. *Renfield*, *The Last Voyage of the Demeter*, and Robert Eggers' *Nosferatu* are all poised to welcome quite a few fans with fresh eyes and new appreciation for the Count at his most wicked.

The same kudos goes out to Tal Minear and the entire incredible *Re: Dracula* crew whose podcast brings extra incentive to hop on the read-along bandwagon. Every entry is more gripping than the last, breathing true character and care into one of my favorite novels in a way I don't think it's experienced in several lifetimes. The same team is poised to tackle an audio drama read straight from the pages of *Carmilla* and my ears are already tingling in anticipation.

I have to thank Polidori and Stoker once again, for the obvious reasons, but also Arthur Conan Doyle, M.R. James, and Aleksey Konstantinovich Tolstoy for offering up more than the usual spread of 'vampire does some vampire things,' that saturated the bloodsucker boom of their era. Without them, I'd be stuck sending 'Quinn Morse' after a bunch of cookie cutter killer cadavers. Or possibly handing him a saw to go prune some fearsome foliage ala Phil Robinson and Ulric Daubeny's hematophagous trees. I guess we'll save that for the sequel.

Most of all, I'd like to thank you. If you picked up this little book, whether you gave it your time in bursts, in skims, or an up-close page-by-page perusal, *thank you*.

From the bottom of my heart, beating or otherwise.

About the Author

C.R. Kane lives in a state of denial with a growing collection of novelty mugs, books read and unread, too many unused journals, and enough scary movies to fill up a dresser. A longtime casual scribbler of supernatural stories, they've occasionally churned out a few shorts for anthologies like *Strange Little Girls*, *Offbeat: Nine Spins on Song*, and *99 Tiny Terrors*, but has mostly kept their assorted horrors to themselves. When not writing, C.R. Kane can be found lurking, skulking, haunting, creeping, and generally pestering in whatever shadow is most convenient. There are links to most of those shadows on my site, seearcanescribbles.com